D1035841

CAPITAL QUEERS

BY FRED HUNTER

The Alex Reynolds Series
Government Gay
Federal Fag
Capital Queers

The Jeremy Ransom/Emily Charters Series
Presence of Mind
Ransom for Our Sins
Ransom for an Angel
Ransom for a Holiday
Ransom for a Killing

CAPITAL QUEERS

Fred Hunter

ST. MARTIN'S PRESS
NEW YORK

Library of Congress Cataloging-in-Publication Data

Hunter, Fred.
    Capital queers: an Alex Reynolds mystery / by Fred Hunter.—
1st ed.
      p.   cm.
    ISBN 0-312-20463-9
    I. Title.
PS3558.U476C36   1999
813'.54—dc21   99-21751
                                           CIP

First Edition: June 1999

10 9 8 7 6 5 4 3 2 1

For John, John, and especially, John

With apologies to Wilkie Collins.

CAPITAL QUEERS

The moon was higher than he would have liked, casting too much light on the street where the endless neon had been extinguished for the night. He ducked into a depression covered with a sheet of metal. He took this to be the entrance to a shop, closed due to the hour. The man pressed himself against the metal, which gave a little with his weight. The street, normally teeming with human masses, was deserted, though the man still felt as if in the darkness of the myriad of shadows and crevasses silent figures watched his every move.

He shivered and peered more closely into the shadows of the shops. He thought feverishly that this city was a bizarre conglomeration of architectural styles, with modern high-rises having sprouted up between ancient structures: a nightmare of hotels and temples. With a sudden stab of irreverence, he thought he might as well be in Washington. But no, even Washington didn't go back this far.

He strained his ears, listening intently for sounds of pursuit. He had hoped he'd be able to obtain the object without being seen, but barring that, without being recognized. But he'd been clumsy. He'd been heard. And the alarm was sounded before he was even fully out of the building. He wasn't sure how many of them had taken off after him, but knew it was more than a few. He thought if he could only make it back to the boat he'd be safe. The object seemed to pulsate in his pocket. He glanced down at it, then realized it was his heart pounding in his chest. Maybe the effort hadn't been worth it. Then again, it would be worth it, if he got away.

He sighed. He couldn't hear the sound of footsteps any more, like the ones he'd heard clamoring up the stairs after him, accompanied by shouts of anger.

He was just about to step out into the street when he heard, faintly at first, the sound of someone approaching hurriedly. He glanced up at the moon and silently cursed it. With all its reflected light he'd be a sitting duck where he stood. And these people would not settle simply for getting the object back: They would exact their revenge. He knew what that would be.

As quietly as he could, he pressed against the corrugated metal behind him, but it would not give way any more than it had. He carefully slipped along the ramshackle structures, looking for any opening through which he could disappear. At last he came upon a lane that opened between two of the shops: a sort of alleyway that snaked off between more buildings. He ducked down the alley, thinking it would at least temporarily confuse his pursuers, and stole quietly a few hundred feet from the opening.

He paused and listened. Footsteps approached from a distance down the street, quickly at first, then slowly as they reached the entrance down which the man had fled. The pursuer hesitated. After a few seconds, the footsteps resumed, coming in the man's direction. His pursuer had turned down the alley. With mounting panic, the man hurried along the twists and turns of the narrow lane, trying doors whenever he dared pause long enough to do it, which wasn't often. At last, his hand lighted upon a door handle that gave at his touch. He stopped, pushed the door open as quietly as he could, and slipped inside, closing the door behind him.

He was now sweating profusely, and having difficulty catching his breath. He pressed his ear against the door and listened. Footsteps rushed past the door and quickly faded off into the distance. However, the man didn't move away from the door. He continued to listen to see if his pursuer would return.

The room into which he'd fled was very dark, illuminated only slightly by the moonlight filtering in through the dirt-encrusted window high up on the wall to his right. Hearing nothing, he pulled a soiled handkerchief from his pocket and mopped his forehead. He spent a minute trying to decide what to do next, whether to remain in this unknown place of refuge for a while, or try to make it back to the boat. Neither option seemed safe. He didn't know when people would start to arrive for work, in whatever business was conducted here, but he knew it wouldn't be long. People in this country start work so damned early.

At last he decided he'd have to stay where he was, at least for the time being. It was too risky to try to go anywhere until the chase had died down. And perhaps when people began to fill the streets he wouldn't be so noticeable. Then again, he knew that he could easily be picked out of a crowd in this God-forsaken country. Or maybe not: There were plenty of American tourists. Maybe . . . just maybe . . . the men at the temple hadn't gotten a good look at him.

He mopped his brow again and sighed. As he stuffed the handkerchief back in his pocket, he turned from the door for the first time.

In the darkness across the room, several pairs of eyes glimmered in his direction.

He screamed.

ONE

I don't like dogs. Actually, it's not that I don't like them, I'm just not what dog lovers insist on calling a "dog person." This is their way of saying that I'm somehow sadly shortchanged in the gene pool and am missing one of the essential joys of life—like having a perky bundle of fur sticking its cold nose in my crotch at four in the morning.

My husband, Peter Livesay, is a dog person and my mother, being British, has a relationship that borders on telepathic with all canines. It was for this reason that custody of a five-year-old West Highland Terrier named Muffin fell to us when our friends Mason LaPere and Ryan Morton went to Washington, D.C. to attend a festive gay-pride parade. Mother spent the week teaching Muffin some much needed manners (since he came from an over-indulgent home), and I spent the week removing the hems of my pants from his teeth.

I was less than sorrowful when Mason and Ryan returned, and I was looking forward to the dinner they were throwing for us by way of thank you. Actually, I was looking forward even more to delivering the nappy-haired little mongrel back into their hands. Mother begged off the dinner, claiming that she'd be glad to have a little time to herself, away from the three of us (she was already lumping the dog in with Peter and me). Personally, I suspect she'd become attached to the thing, and though she knew there was never any possibility of our keeping him, she was a little too sad about it to want to face handing him over.

"Will you hurry up?" I said impatiently to Peter as he brushed his wavy hair for what seemed like the fifth time. Peter's not really vain, but he pays an awful lot of attention to his hair.

"Just can't wait to give over little Muffin, can you?" he said, his reflection smiling at me in the bathroom mirror. "Do you really hate him that much?"

"I don't hate the *dog*—it's his name. What were they thinking of? They branded him for life. Like people who name their sons Lance, and then expect them to be straight."

Peter laughed as he laid down his brush and took one more look at himself in the mirror. I marvelled once again at the contrast between us: Peter's olive skin as opposed to my fairness, his very dark brown hair next to my blondness, and his natural calm next to my perennial fidgeting. It's his serenity that amazes me the most, especially because, ever since we became part-timers for the CIA, I've certainly given him enough to fidget about.

"What are you so nervous for?" he said. I noticed for the first time that his expression had turned to concern.

"Nothing," I said, leaving the bathroom. Peter followed, switching off the light behind us.

"Is it because of Mason?"

I stopped in my tracks. I guess that's what comes from being an old married couple. Peter sometimes demonstrates that he knows me so well it makes me comfortable and uncomfortable at the same time.

"In a way, but not like you think," I replied.

"I wasn't thinking anything bad. I just thought it was because of his HIV."

When he came right out and said it, it sounded bad.

"But it's not what you think," I repeated anxiously.

"Honey, I know you're not afraid of people with HIV. You've

certainly been around them enough. What makes Mason different?"

"I don't know. I think it's because I've known him so long—I don't understand what's going on with him, and it makes me nervous."

"How do you mean?"

I sucked in my lips for a second or two, trying to think of how to put it. "Have you noticed that he never really says anything about it? I mean, about his condition."

Peter shrugged. "He probably discusses it with Ryan."

"Yeah, but I've known him for years. When I'm around him now I feel like there's a rhino in the room and we're all pretending it's not there. I don't know, I feel like grabbing him by the shoulders and shaking him. Do you understand that?"

Peter's green eyes surveyed my face lovingly for a moment before he said, "Yes, I do. But you know he has to deal with his illness in his own way and in his own time."

"Yeah, I know. So do I. And someday I might have to say something to him about it." Peter's forehead creased just slightly. I smiled at him and added, "But not tonight."

"Good boy," he said, giving the upper part of my back a quick rub with his palm. Then, trying to lessen my anxiety, he added, "You know, I think what's really worrying you is the prospect of seeing Mason's collection again."

I heaved an exaggerated sigh, rolled my eyes, and said, "Oh, please, God, spare us! And don't you say anything that'll get him started on the subject, either."

Peter smiled and began to whistle "Oh, You Beautiful Doll" as we descended the stairs. I was just about to smack the side of his head when I spotted Mother by the door, beaming down at the dog who gazed back up at her with sparkling eyes, his tail wagging so violently I expected his ass to lift off the ground. Mother has that effect on most men. Around the dog's neck was a tacky rhinestone necklace that Mason had bought for him because he said it made the dog look like Zsa Zsa Gabor. The weird part was that it did.

"Be sure to tell them that he's been a very, very good boy while he's been our guest, and that we're glad to have him back any time," she said, handing the leash to Peter.

At the end of our sidewalk, the dog gave a jerk to the leash that momentarily stopped us. He was turned around and looking back at the door to our house, where mother stood waving.

"Ta, Muffin. You be a good boy!"

Peter tugged at the leash and I rolled my eyes again.

"Muffin!" cried Mason as he opened the door. He cooed at the thing like an insipid parent talking to a newborn baby. "Muffy, sweetie! You're back! Did you miss me? Of course you did!"

The dog licked Mason's face as Mason planted several little kisses on his head. I didn't think I was going to be able to eat dinner.

"Thank you so, so much for taking care of our little Muffy," he said as he led us into the living room.

Mason and Ryan lived in the sprawling first-floor apartment of an enormous two-flat that they owned. They rented the upstairs to a lipstick lesbian and her partner, a flannel dyke, both of whom I'd met a couple of times at parties.

Their apartment was a study in how to decorate for opposites. The decor was Southwestern, with pictures of deserts, adobe abodes, and Native-American pottery on the walls. The hardwood floor was covered by a huge woven rug with a design that Mason always referred to as "Navajo-lite." The whole place looked just slightly too butch for Mason, and just a little too pastel for Ryan. For the two of them together it was perfect.

"Is that our guests?" called a deep voice from the kitchen.

"Yes, sweetie," Mason replied.

"I'll be out there in a minute. I'm up to my armpits in noodles."

Mason smiled and with exaggerated weariness said, "He's sooo *de classe*. I'm surprised I can get him to eat with utensils."

While Mason continued his sloppy reunion with the dog, I used the opportunity to examine our friend. Mason was one of the few people with whom I'd remained in contact from high school. He had been losing his dishwater-blond hair for years, but the loss had been accelerated recently by his frequent bouts of chemotherapy. Though he'd always been reedy, he was beginning to look gaunt. Fortunately, on him the increased thinness, coupled with his wispy voice and general dreaminess, went together in a way that looked natural.

"I'd better put you down now, little baby," said Mason, lovingly setting the dog on the floor. Muffin was immediately off to the kitchen, yapping all the way.

"Whoa, Nelly!" cried Ryan from the kitchen.

"Have a seat," said Mason, motioning us to the earth-toned couch. He sat in one of the two matching chairs across from us. Grouped like this in the midst of all the Southwestern accoutrements, I half expected him to start a campfire on the coffee table. "Can I get you anything to drink?"

We both declined for the time being, saying we'd have something with dinner.

"Was Muffy any trouble?" Mason's glowing face seemed to imply he already knew that his baby couldn't possibly have caused us a moment's distress.

"Not for—" I started to say "not for Mother and Peter," but Peter stopped me with an unexpected kick to my shin.

"Ow!"

"Sorry, honey, my foot slipped."

I turned back to Mason and said, "No, of course not. He was no trouble at all. Mother said he can come back any time."

"She's a dear."

"Everybody thinks that," I said. "It's the accent."

"It's too bad she couldn't make it tonight."

"She was heartbroken at the thought of losing Muffin," said Peter with a sly glance in my direction.

"Really?" said Mason, whose gaze drifted over my head, lost for a moment in dog lover's reverie. "I missed him. But I knew that you guys would take good care of him."

"Well, Mother gets most of the credit."

"Thank you for watering the plants and taking in the mail. It was so sweet of you. We would've had the girls do it," he glanced at the ceiling, "but Ronnie's always working and Linda's . . . well, Linda. Done up like a drag queen and just as unreliable."

We laughed. Mason could get away with saying something like that in any company because he'd done his share of drag.

"Oh! I forgot to bring your keys back," I said, giving my forehead a gentle slap.

"Hold onto them," Mason said with a tired smile, "Who knows? We might become world travelers."

"So, how've you been feeling?" I asked. Peter shot me a glance.

"Oh . . . great. And we had a wonderful time while we were away!" Mason replied with a flap of his hand, apparently meant to dismiss the subject of his health. "I can't wait to tell you all about the pride parade. It was a hoot! Although, between you, me, and the lamp post, it's gotten *way* too political. I long for the tacky glamor of yesteryear." He sighed.

At that point, Ryan Morton walked into the room. He was a stark contrast to Mason. Ryan is very straight-looking with short black hair, thick eyebrows and thick lips, and muscles that have been finely tuned at a health club. When he came into the room he was sporting his omnipresent White Sox cap, always worn backward, faded black shorts, and an equally faded green T-shirt that bore the words "Hang on there, Gecko" with a picture of the offending lizard. He looked like the kind of guy who'd be bashing Mason rather than making love to him. But whenever you caught Ryan looking at Mason, there were stars in his eyes. The adoration between them was always evident, but even more so now that Mason's health was in danger.

"Anybody hungry?" said Ryan, "Spaghetti's on!"

Mason spent the dinner describing in excruciatingly funny detail the pride parade they'd attended in Washington. He related a story of one particular senator whose placement in the parade was temporarily interrupted when he spent a little too long shaking hands with the mincing masses of potential voters along the parade route. When he turned back, expecting to find his limousine, he instead found a float full of drag queens done up to look like Lisa Marie. Mason did a near-perfect (according to Ryan) imitation of the famed senator's plasticized smile melting in horror and confusion as he then lurched quickly up the street like a drunken sailor in pursuit of his limo.

"It was the only truly amusing part of our program," Mason concluded.

"It's a shame that it's all become so political," said Ryan, unknowingly echoing what Mason had said earlier. He paused for a sip of wine then added, "but then again, it's a shame that it had to."

There was a sudden silence. Although Ryan is usually incredibly sensitive to Mason's feelings, I don't think he realized all the ramifications of this simple statement. The parades had started to change as the community had become politically galvanized in response to the AIDS epidemic. The mention of this was like throwing a tarp over the proceedings. Mason was staring at his wineglass with a glazed smile on his face, choosing to ignore the silence. Ryan looked absolutely stricken. After a moment he cleared his throat.

"We did a lot of sightseeing while we were there."

"And some shopping," Mason chimed in, happy that the momentary glitch had passed.

I glanced at Peter, who smiled back at me, knowing that for Mason, shopping most likely meant there was an addition to his collection.

"Did you go to all the monuments?" Peter asked. It was difficult to hide my gratitude at his pursuing the first option.

"Yeah," said Ryan eagerly, "It was great!"

"We saw *all* the monuments, the Lincoln Memorial, the Washington Monument, everything! I felt just like Judy Holliday in *Born Yesterday!*" Mason was quiet for a minute, lost in a memory. The smile faded from his thin face and was replaced by an expression far more reverent than anything I'd ever seen there before. "You know, it makes you feel so small." He stopped as if these few words would explain everything.

"What do you mean?" Ryan prompted lovingly.

"Being there—seeing all the historical stuff: the Declaration of Independence and the Constitution and everything. It makes you feel like the country was founded by something bigger than any of us . . . and bigger than what we've become. . . . I mean, than what the government's become."

Ryan continued to gaze at his lover, his forehead creasing with concern.

"I'm sorry, Masey," I said, adopting my familiar name for him, "I still don't get it."

He turned his sunken eyes toward me and I noticed for the first time that the blue in them seemed a little faded. But he brightened at last, the pensiveness replaced by a smile as he said, "But the best part about our nation's capital is that I managed to find the *perfect* addition to my collection!"

Oh Lord, here it comes, I thought.

Mason pushed back his chair and said, "Alex, you'll absolutely *love* her. She's another one of my Traviata girls!"

I got up to follow him as Ryan said, "I'll clear, honey," to which Peter added, "I'll help." I would have been proud of my husband's undying courtesy if I hadn't been so sure that he was doing it to avoid the same fate as mine.

I tossed a helpless look over my shoulder toward my helpmate as I followed Mason down the creaking hardwood floor to their guest room, where his collection was housed. Mason threw the door open with a tired flourish and switched on the floor lamp. It instantly threw into rather ghostly illumination the several shelves full of dolls that lined his walls. I have to admit that his collection, which includes over three dozen various and obviously expensive dolls, is very impressive. But I'd seen them before, and the way Mason doted on them set my teeth on edge.

"As you know," he said, adopting his fey museum-director persona, "the Barbie portion of our program is one of my pride and joys."

Mason pointed to one after the other. "The Wedding Day Barbie, Dream Date Barbie, Star Dream Barbie, Black Barbie—from the all–dolls–are–created–equal period of doll making—my holiday Barbie in red. . . . Doesn't she look just like a blood-soaked snowflake? And of course, my favorite: spuj Barbie." He plucked from the shelf a doll with the same vacuous, perky expression as the others, but she was dressed like a valley girl trapped in a kitchen-sink drama. Mason straightened her dress and set her back in her stand.

"Of course, you know all the others," he said, waving his hands at the dozens of dolls as he continued toward the opposite end of the shelves. "Trulamae, Dolly Madison, all the girls!" I was relieved that it appeared he wouldn't be doting over the whole collection this evening, because once you get him started, it's hard to stop him. Like most collectors he's developed an eye for the real thing. Among others, he has a Deanna Durbin doll, a Scarlet O'Hara (one of his prize possessions), as well as a Snow White that's over fifty years old, and has skin that was painted a curiously dark color.

"But of course, these are my faves! My Traviata girls!"

He reached the end of the shelves and struck a Vanna White pose, his hands fluttering. He'd aptly named these the Traviata girls: They were each dressed in elaborate gowns of velvet or taffeta in a multitude of colors. They had ceramic heads, intricately coiffed hair, delicately painted faces, and glass eyes, all of which taken together made them look eerily human. You got the feeling that when you left the room they'd break into a rousing rendition of "Libiamo." I've always admired the artistry of these particular dolls, while at the same time silently acknowledging that they give me the creeps.

"This is our new addition," he said, gently lifting from the shelf the most astoundingly lifelike doll I'd ever seen: She was wearing a deep red, velvet gown with a matching hat, and had a lace kerchief pinned at her neck. But it was the head that was so striking: The hair was swept back in a way that made it look quite natural, and the eyes and face were so perfectly executed that they were unnervingly lifelike.

"She's beautiful," I said. I made the noises of admiration which were expected of me, but it was all I could do not to shudder. I just knew I'd be seeing this alarming little woman in my nightmares, but in them she'd be wielding a teeny-weeny razor blade.

"I got her in a fancy doll shop in Georgetown."

He fussed with the doll's dress for a moment, straightening it and smoothing it with his fingers, then he swept her hair back gently, as if to brush it out of her eyes.

"You know," he said absently, "there's something I've been meaning to talk to you about."

I continued to watch him as he picked a stray piece of lint from the back of the doll's dress, then carefully placed her back in her stand.

"Alex?"

"I'm sorry," I said, turning red, "I thought you were talking to the doll."

Mason turned his narrow face toward mine and pursed his lips, the corners of his mouth just barely rising.

"I don't hold conversations with them," he said.

"I know that," I protested, though in truth, it wouldn't have surprised me.

"Well," he said slowly, casting a sad look at the dolls, "if anything should ever happen to me, I want you to have my girls."

I blinked and my mouth dropped open just a little before I could stop it. Ironically enough, after telling Peter how uncomfortable I felt with Mason's avoidance of the subject of his health, I was really unprepared for this direct assault.

"You what?"

"You've always appreciated them. . . . At least, you've always been willing to come and look at them with me. I want you to have them."

"Mason, that's really . . . nice . . . but I don't think you should

13

talk like this. You look great. You'll be with us for years."

He let out an abbreviated snort and said, "Let's face it, sweety, I'm fading fast. I may have a while, I may not. I don't dwell on it. But I'm not an idiot."

"Wouldn't you rather leave them to Ryan? After all . . ."

"Oh, my butch husband!" Mason replied with a grin, "He's so sweet. But you know, he just tolerates them. I mean, he may admire them in some way, but not the way you do. If I collected baseball cards I wouldn't hesitate to leave them to him."

"He might surprise you."

I wasn't saying this just because I didn't want the collection, although it did make me really uncomfortable knowing that I didn't share Mason's love for the things. It was because I knew that people become very peculiar when a loved one dies, and I thought Ryan might attach a lot more importance to Mason's collection in death than he had in life.

"No, no," Mason said, still smiling. He moved to the middle of the shelves, spread out his arms toward the dolls, and said in an imitation of Maggie Smith in *The Prime of Miss Jean Brodie*, "These are all my girls, and I love them. I want you to have them when I'm gone. You're the only one who'll keep them for me, and take care of them the way they should be. Someday . . . someday Ryan may meet someone else . . . and maybe he won't want to have any reminders of his old love around. . . ."

"You know that's not true," I said.

He smiled at me indulgently, letting me know that I was interrupting his performance. ". . . and he'll be forced to get rid of my girls somehow." Mason turned to me with the most knowing, twisted smile I've ever seen on his face. "You, on the other hand, would be under no such constraints. Giving them to you would insure their safety. Knowing how much they meant to me, you would never . . . ever . . . get rid of them."

I narrowed my eyes at him, and couldn't help giving him a little smile of admiration. Apparently he'd always known that my interest in his collection amounted to little more than indulging him. Mason was not incapable of irony, even when it came to his own end. He'd hit on the perfect plan for getting back at me. What he said was true: The dolls would live forever in my care because I'd be too goddamn sentimental to get rid of them at any price, knowing how much they'd meant to him.

He wasn't willing me the dolls, he was cursing me with the damn things! And from the look on his face, he was enjoying himself.

"But you *wanted* him to talk about it," said Peter as we walked home.

"I didn't want him to talk about leaving me those demonic little icons," I replied.

Peter couldn't help but laugh at this. "Mason always did know how to go straight for the gut."

"But you know, I wasn't kidding when I told him I thought Ryan would want them."

His smile faded a little. "I know, and I think you're right."

We walked on in silence for a couple of minutes, then I said, "So tell me, honey, if I died, would you be sentimental about my things?"

The left corner of his mouth slid upward, giving his profile a sly cast. "I promise that if I ever lose you I'll have your Mold-A-Rama souvenir likeness of Mt. Rushmore put on a chain which I'll wear around my neck for the rest of my days."

"Jerk," I said, giving his shoulder a playful slap. "That souvenir will come back to haunt you."

"It already does."

TWO

On the following Thursday, Peter came home early from work so we could have an early dinner and catch a movie. This was an event for us because we were actually going to go *out* to a movie, rather than watching one of the four hundred we have in our video library.

We were just sitting down to dinner when the phone rang. My two loved ones looked down at their plates, feigning deafness.

"Oh, no, I'll get it," I said, giving Peter's shoulder a talonlike squeeze as I passed him.

"Hello?" I said into the phone.

"Alex?" The voice sounded out of breath and quavery. I just barely recognized it as belonging to Ryan.

"Ryan? What is it?"

"It's Mason. He's dead."

I was struck dumb. It's one of the ironies of terminal illness that death is always unexpected, even when you expect it. I glanced over at Mother and Peter, who had both stopped eating and were staring at me anxiously, as if they could sense that whatever it was was bad news. Like most people in shock, the first thing that came out of my mouth was idiotic.

"But . . . he seemed so healthy the other night."

"Alex . . . it's . . . Can you come over? Please?"

"We'll be right there."

Mother decided to stay home, clear the table, and get our guest room—the one that serves as my office—ready.

"You make sure he comes home with you. He shouldn't be alone," she said as we left.

Peter and I walked the two blocks to Ryan and Mason's apartment, silently dreading whatever we were walking into. What we *did* find was what we least expected: There was a squad car sitting in front of the building, and another car double-parked beside it. I thought I recognized it as an "unmarked" car of the type that detectives use.

Ryan was sitting on the cement steps while a man stood over him asking him questions, to which Ryan didn't appear to be paying much attention. Ryan was wearing jeans and a flannel shirt and his inevitable Sox cap. His knees were together and his heels turned outward, which despite his heavy five-o'clock shadow made him look like a little boy. He was clutching a Raggedy Ann doll for dear life. Muffin sat at the bottom of the steps glaring up at the stranger as if unsure whether to simply bark or go ahead and attack.

As we approached this scene, Ryan looked up at us and said, "It was one of his favorites. He wouldn't have admitted to it, you know, but he loved it."

It took me a moment to realize that he was referring to the limp doll.

"What happened?" said Peter.

The man slid his hand in front of Ryan's face, a gesture meant to caution him against answering. He then looked at us and said, "Who're you?"

"I'm Alex Reynolds, this is Peter Livesay. And you are . . . ?"

"Detective Billings," he said in a midwestern drawl. It sounded manufactured, as if he were working at sounding like a detective. He had a complexion the color of powdered sugar, a face that was rounding out and looked in danger of bulging out, and black eyes that I'm sure seemed beadier than they were because of the size of his face. He had brown hair that needed washing and a brown suit that needed cleaning.

I turned to Ryan, "When you said Mason was dead, we thought . . ."

" 'Scuse me," said Billings, "What are you doing here?"

"Ryan and Mason are friends of ours."

"Friends," replied Billings in a tone I didn't care for.

"Um-hm," said Peter, folding his arms over his chest, "What's the problem?"

"We have an investigation going on here, so you're going to have to wait to talk to Mr. Morton here."

I looked at Ryan again. "Didn't Mason die of . . . I thought you said he died."

Ryan looked up at me with watery eyes and I thought I detected a slight shake of his head.

"I found him," he said.

I said to Billings, "Are you with homicide?"

"Uh huh."

"Well, what's going on?"

"Your friend here says he came home and found his buddy dead. That's all there is to it."

"Dead," Peter repeated flatly.

"Murdered."

"There was . . ." Ryan stammered, ". . . blood . . . and all the dolls. All his dolls . . ."

I noticed that Billings had transferred his smirk from us to Ryan, and it made me want to break his face.

"He was killed?" I said stupidly. "By who?"

"We were just about to take your friend here into Area Headquarters to have a talk about that."

"Take him in?" I really couldn't erase the incredulity from my voice. "You don't mean you think he had something to do with it!"

"In cases like this, it's a definite possibility." The look on his face told me exactly what "cases like this" meant.

"He would never hurt Mason." My voice cracked with anger.

"Um . . ." He made a dumb show of pondering this. It really was going to be difficult not to strike this idiot, though I've never resorted to violence myself and I knew that if I chose this moment to start, I would definitely be making matters a lot worse. ". . . maybe not. Maybe after we talk to him for a while, we'll find out whether or not he coulda done it."

"So you're arresting him?" said Peter, trying to force the detective's hand.

Billings smiled. "We just want to talk to him. So far."

"You don't have to take him in for that. Not unless you're arresting him," said Peter.

Billings's face hardened, making him look as if he was cast in plaster. "Might go better for him if we take him in."

"It would be easier to abuse him here," Peter shot back. "There're so few people around."

"Peter . . ." I said cautioningly. I'm not fond of the police, either, but I didn't see any reason to provoke them.

Billings screwed his face up at us, once again putting on an act of pondering something, then added, "Hmmm, you know, I'd also appreciate it if the two of you would join us."

Peter and I glanced at each other. He was as astonished as I was. "Us? What for?"

"Well, if you're friends of these guys, you might be able to help us figure out who did this."

"How in the hell should we know who did it?" I said, "We just got here!"

"You guys know each other, don't you?"

He made it sound like he thought all faggots knew each other, the way some people, upon learning that Mother is British, ask her if she knows Emma Thompson.

Peter tilted his head a little sideways, his eyes narrowing. "So you're arresting us, too?"

Billings shook his head. "Not arresting—we'd just like you to come to headquarters and . . . talk to us."

19

"And if we refuse?" I said rashly.

His smile grew broader and more menacing. "Hmmm, well, you ever heard of this thing called obstructing justice?"

"I've heard of it," Peter replied. "I've never personally experienced it."

Billings clucked his tongue. "If we thought you knew something that might help us solve this murder and you were holding it back, it wouldn't be good."

I'd hate to say I was astonished for fear of looking more naive than I really am. But frankly, in my everyday life I really don't have much of an occasion to run into any sort of discrimination or intimidation, other than the occasional threat to my life from foreign agents. That's one of the advantages of being six feet tall. So even though I often hear horror stories from my friends about how they've been treated, I seldom come in contact with any of it directly.

I looked Billings squarely in the eye, shrugged with resignation and said, "Oh, we'd be glad to come with you." I looked at Peter and added, "It'll give us a chance to say hi to Frank, won't it Peter?"

"Frank?" said Billings.

"Frank O'Neil. He's, uh . . . What was his title again, Peter?"

"Commander," Peter replied simply.

"Oh, yeah. Commander. He'll probably still be there, won't he? It's early yet."

Billings looked at me doubtfully and said, "You know Frank O'Neil?"

"Well, sort of," I said innocently, "He dates my mother."

Billings looked at me as if he couldn't believe I *had* a mother.

"Well, now, Alex," Peter said, "to be perfectly accurate, they *dated* each other. Past tense. But I believe they're still quite close, aren't they?"

"Oh, yes."

I had the feeling that Billings was trying to decide which course would get him in the most trouble. After a long pause, he said with a degree of contrition that I was sure would send stock

20

in Rolaids soaring, "Well . . . if you know Frank than I'm sure you know how much he'd want you to help us . . . sort this out."

"Anything to help," I said. I didn't even try to hide my own smirk.

Peter and I waited alone in an interrogation room at Area Headquarters. It was a drab room, furnished solely with a table and chairs that can best be described as shanty-modern. I could only imagine what the fluorescent lighting was doing to my complexion.

It was Billings's misfortune that we ran into Frank almost the moment we were through the door. Frank is tall and masculine, in his late fifties, and aging just as gracefully as my mother. He's become more rugged-looking as he's gotten older, rather than developing that paunch and hang-dog look so common in middle-aged cops. I mean men.

I'm not sure whether Frank's astonished expression stemmed from our being led into headquarters by one of his men, or the fact that we had that damn dog in tow, since we'd insisted on bringing Muffin with us for fear he'd be lost otherwise. To Billings's obvious dismay, Frank took charge of us and led us to an interrogation room. The one thing he did allow was for Ryan to be separated from us.

"I can't say I think much of the way you guys issue invitations," said Peter hotly.

"I don't think Mother will, either," I added, knowing that it would sting.

Frank remained unfazed and asked us what had happened. We gave him all the details with only slight departures into what we thought of the attitude of Detective Billings.

"Not everyone's as liberal as I am," said Frank.

Peter let out a little snort. It was ill-advised, but I couldn't blame him. We both knew that Frank's liberality stretched only as far as his infatuation with my mother. Fortunately, that was pretty far.

After allowing me to call home and let Mother know what

was going on, Frank excused himself, saying he would check on the status of the case with Billings. As we waited for his return, Muffin stood on all fours with his right side pressed against my leg, as if prepared to protect me from something. Peter and I sat in a fuming silence that went unbroken until I said, "I never, ever thought I'd see the day that I'd be glad Frank dated Mother."

"It's not the first time you've been glad you know him, or are you forgetting that unfortunate Russian affair?"

"I stand corrected."

A few minutes later Frank returned, his expression pretty much vacant.

"Well," he said, turning a chair around and straddling it, "it looks like your friend—"

"Ryan," I interrupted. I was getting a little sick of them referring to him by something other than his name.

Frank paused pregnantly before continuing. "Ryan . . . says he came home from work and found his lover dead, that he called the police, then he called you."

"Do you have any reason to think he's lying?" I asked.

"Not yet," said Frank, with a cautionary glance in my direction. "I gather from Billings that even *he* could tell that the guy'd been dead for more than a little while when they arrived, so it would appear that Ryan's telling the truth."

"*Appear*," said Peter.

Frank took a deep breath, let it out, and said, "You know, I wish you guys would keep in mind that I'm not the enemy."

After a beat, Peter said, "Sorry. But it's not like we're universally loved here."

"Nobody is," said Frank. "So, along with the length of time he's been dead, there's the method. It's doesn't ring right."

"How was he killed?" I asked.

"Ritual-style."

"You mean he was shot in the head?"

Frank shook his head. "Nope. He was eviscerated."

"*Eviscerated*," said Peter, his brows snaking toward the bridge of his nose.

"Stuck a knife in his stomach, then—"

"I know what it means," said Peter wryly, "I'm just surprised you do."

Frank shot him an angry glance, but didn't blow up. "It isn't the type of thing you see every day."

"Who would do such a thing?" I asked incredulously.

"Gangs, cults," Frank replied with a shrug. "Somebody trying to prove something or maybe somebody trying to scare somebody." He paused for a moment, then added, "You guys don't happen to know if he was into anything out of the ordinary, do you?" He turned to Peter and added with an air of getting him back, "I realize that's a relative term for the two of you."

Peter disappointed him by answering calmly, "The only thing out of the ordinary that Mason did was collect dolls. And even that's not very odd."

"I guess," said Frank doubtfully.

"And you know . . ." I started to say, but stopped short just in time.

"What?" said Frank after a pause.

"Nothing."

Frank looked at me a minute, then shook his head like a father who's just discovered that his son wears panty hose.

"So you have those reasons to believe Ryan isn't the killer," Peter said, in a not-to-subtle attempt to deflect attention from me. "Do you have any reason to believe he *is* involved?"

Frank gave an abbreviated nod. "Aside from the fact that murder is usually committed by . . ." He looked at me, then at Peter. It was a moment before I realized he was trying to think of a word he'd be comfortable using for a homosexual spouse.

"By the husband?" I said flatly.

He cleared his throat. "Domestic homicide is usually committed by someone close."

"That's it?" said Peter.

"No. I started to say that aside from that, there's the dolls. All those dolls—most of them, at least—were busted."

"So what?"

"So, that would make it seem somebody was pretty angry. And somebody close to him that got angry would know that breaking those dolls would hurt him, don't you think?"

"Actually . . . yes," I said, unable to resist the truth.

"Does this mean you're going to hold him?" Peter asked.

"We have to at least check on his alibi before letting him go."

"His *alibi?*" said Peter. Even I was beginning to wish he'd wipe that tone from his voice.

"I mean check to see that he really did stay at work, that he didn't disappear for any length of time. If he has witnesses that he stayed put, it doesn't necessarily clear him but it would mean we could let him go for the time being."

"That should be easy enough," I said. "He works for the phone company. I'm sure they watch his every move. They can probably give you a tape of it."

Frank rose from his chair, spun it around and pushed it under the table. "You guys going to wait for him? It might take a while."

"I think we'd better," said Peter.

"Whatever you think is best," said Frank evenly, though it was clear that Peter's choice of words hadn't been lost on him. "You can wait in here, if you like, unless we need the room for something else."

"Thanks," I said.

Frank popped the door open, but paused in the opening, his eyes trained on the floor. "By the way, how's Jean doing?"

"She's waiting for us," I replied pointedly.

Frank sighed again and left the room, closing the door behind him.

Mother was waiting at the door when we arrived home. She gave Ryan a warm, sympathetic hug. He wrapped his arms around her, with tears brimming from beneath his long, dark lashes. All the while he had grasped in his large palm the mitt of the doll, which dangled from his hand like a dead thing. Mother then led him up to the guest room and made sure that he was comfortable before leaving him.

While they were upstairs, Peter asked me, "What were you going to tell Frank?"

"Huh?"

"When he asked us if Mason did anything out of the ordinary, you started to say something, then stopped."

"Oh. I almost told him that Mason had AIDS, but I thought the better of it."

"Why?"

"For a couple of reasons. I don't it's right to reveal someone's AIDS status."

"Even if he's dead?"

I shrugged. It wasn't something I'd had a lot of time to give rational thought to, but even in death the idea of disclosing someone's status bothered me. "I had another reason, which I realize isn't a very reasonable one: After the way we were treated by Billings, I wasn't in any big hurry to help the police. Even Frank."

"Has it occurred to you that Mason's murder might have something to do with his having AIDS?"

"How?"

He shrugged. "You know how incredibly paranoid some people still are on the subject. Maybe somebody's decided to act as some sort of vigilante."

"Who would do something like that?"

"Don't be naive. Any number of nuts. But the most logical thing that comes to mind is that maybe Mason passed it to someone before he knew he was infected. Maybe that someone didn't take the news very well."

That was something that hadn't occurred to me. It sickened me to think of how much sense it made.

"Then it's a really good thing I didn't tell him."

"Why?"

"Who do you think they'd think would be the most likely person to be angry about something like that?"

Peter turned his head toward the ceiling, looking in the general direction of the guest room. "Um-hm."

"There's one other problem with your idea," I said.

25

Peter turned back to me and said, "What?"

"The method of murder," I said, trying not to sound like Frank when I said it. "If a former lover—"

"Or present one—"

". . . All right," I conceded, "or a present one, or even some sort of vigilante murdered him because he had AIDS, would they spill so much blood?"

Peter shook his head slowly.

"Not unless they felt they had nothing to fear."

THREE

I awoke the next morning in my usual hazy state, lying on my side toward the middle of the bed where a depression in the mattress seemed to be trying to suck me back into dreamland. I was about to drift off again when I had the sudden and unnerving feeling that I was being watched. I frowned and started to roll over on my back to see who was doing the looking when something extremely cold touched my arm and I leapt up from the bed like a spastic ballerina. There, sitting on the edge of the bed, was Muffin, his ears sticking up like attentive little antennae. He stared at me for a moment, then cocked his head sideways as if I was some sort of interesting specimen. His tail wagged wildly.

"Off!" I said firmly. "Off the bed!"

He cocked his head the other way.

I rolled my eyes, threw on my old, worn-out, baby blue terry cloth robe and headed downstairs to the kitchen, the pint-sized furry shadow following close at my heels.

"There's my darling," said Mother as we entered the room.

Muffin scuttled past me and plopped his butt in front of her, his tail rapidly sweeping a tiny area of the floor. I was embarrassed to realize that Mother was referring to the dog.

"Here you go," she said. She retrieved a gingersnap from a glass jar on the counter, bent down, and held it in front of the dog, who carefully snatched it from her fingers.

"Good boy," said mother. Then she glanced up at me and said, "Oh, hi, luv."

"You could at least acknowledge me *before* the dog," I said, barely moving my lips.

She brushed my cheek with the back of her hand and said, "Don't worry, darling, you'll always be my pet."

I growled.

Peter laughed and choked on a bite of strawberry-jam–laden toast he'd been in the process of chewing. "Good morning," he managed to cough out when he'd gotten hold of himself.

I kissed him on the head, took my seat, and poured myself some tea from the white, ivy-embossed pot that Mother has kept for years for sentimental reasons to which I'm not privy.

"Will you have some toast?" she asked.

"Thanks."

"Did you see Ryan yet this morning?" said Peter.

"No. Hasn't he been down yet?"

"Uh uh. And I didn't look in on him. I didn't want to wake him. God knows he needs all the rest he can get after yesterday."

Mother made a *tsk*ing noise as she stood waiting for the toaster to pop.

"God, this is going to be hard," said Peter.

"And the police have every intention of making it harder," I replied. It crossed my mind that it was too early in the morning to sound so bitter, a belief that was apparently shared by mother if you could go by the glance she shot me. "We *told* you what happened last night . . . about that guy Billings."

"There are sods everywhere," said mother, "but for every Billings there's an O'Neil."

"I know," I said, attempting a conciliatory tone. As mad as I was about the whole thing last night, I still had to admit she was right: Frank O'Neil is about as straight as you can get an arrow, and I mean that in every way possible. If he has any personal prejudices, he has the good grace to keep them hidden.

"I've spoken with Frank this morning," said mother as she pulled the toast from the machine.

"So early?"

"Hmm. I just wanted to find out about the status of things. He couldn't tell me a lot, other than the fact that there was quite a mess in the apartment. There was a lot of blood."

"Was anything stolen?"

"I asked him that. They don't know yet. They'll need someone to look over things and tell them, and of course that'll have to be Ryan. But . . ." Her voice trailed off, and she looked from me to Peter, her expression clearly telling us she didn't exactly want to tell us the next part. I decided to help her out.

"But they don't think it was a robbery."

Mother nodded reluctantly as she put the plate in front of me. "They think it was a *crime passionnel*. At least that's what that Billings person told Frank."

"And I'll bet his penis stood up and nodded when he said it."

"Please, dear, not over breakfast," said mother with a delicate wave of her hand. "Frank did go so far as to say—and now Alex, he didn't sound happy about it when he said it—that this sort of thing usually does turn out to be a crime of passion."

I looked at her a moment. "Well, as long as he wasn't happy about it."

We fell silent. I took a bite of toast then dropped it back on the plate. I wasn't hungry.

"The one good thing he told me was that they've done everything they need to do to Ryan and Mason's apartment, so he can go back there when he's ready."

"God," I said, a rush of conflicting thoughts about how that would feel flooding into my mind.

"Exactly," she said. She sat down and poured herself what I'm sure was at least her third cup of tea. Muffin had followed her back and forth, then laid himself down by her feet once she'd settled. "But you know he can stay here as long as he likes. There's no hurry." She paused, then added, "The only problem is, of course, the police are going to want him to look over things pretty soon."

Peter frowned at her. "And I suppose it's to Ryan's benefit to give the appearance of cooperating in every way."

"Well, Mother, how do you feel about putting in a hard day's work?"

She looked down her aquiline nose at me, brushed the dark bangs from her eyes, and said, "Really, darling."

"It *was* a stupid question."

"What did you have in mind?"

"I thought it might at least make it easier for him if we went over first and tried to clean the place up."

"Good idea. I don't like the idea of leaving Ryan here alone, though. Not with what's happened."

"Don't worry about that," said Peter, "I'll call Art and ask if I can have the day off. I don't think he'll mind."

I was sure he was right. Arthur Dingle is the owner of Farrahut's, the men's clothing store where Peter works when we're not working on one of our all-too-infrequent cases for the CIA. Dingle is very understanding about Peter's unexplained absences. Well, they're not exactly unexplained, but the explanations have been pretty lame, since he couldn't tell his employer the truth. But in recent days it hadn't been a problem. We hadn't heard from Lawrence Nelson, our "boss" at the agency, since our unfortunate interference in a case involving the gay porn industry. Nelson had been more than nice about it, and I'd even gotten the impression he'd been a little proud of our work. But the whole thing had been a cockup from start to finish—so to speak.

I finished my tea in a gulp, pushed the cup and saucer away, and rose from the table. "I'll ask Ryan—see how he feels about our plans."

I went upstairs and knocked lightly on the door, but didn't get a response. After waiting a minute or two I opened the door as quietly as I could and peeked in. Ryan was lying on his side on the day bed. His legs were pulled up in fetal position and his arms were wrapped around Raggedy Ann, but his eyes were open. He looked like he'd been that way all night.

"Can I come in?" I said, taking a tentative step into the room.

He blinked by way of answer. I pulled the chair out from beneath my desk and sat beside him.

"Ryan . . . Mother and I were thinking of going over to your apartment and cleaning up a little. Is that all right with you?"

"Yes." He said it so quietly I almost didn't hear him. He tightened his grip on the doll for a moment, then relaxed it. "Will he be gone?"

"Mason? Yes. I'm sure he will."

He was silent for a moment, then said, "I still can't believe this has happened."

"I know."

"I thought . . . I thought I was prepared to lose him, but not like this."

"I know."

He was silent again. He didn't move. At last he said, "And they think I did this to him, don't they?"

I sighed. "The police don't have much of an imagination."

"I couldn't have done it, but . . ."

"What?" I prompted him softly.

He swallowed hard, and tears formed in his eyes.

"But sometimes I thought . . . I wished he was gone, and that it was all over. You know what I mean?"

"Yes. I do. It was a natural thing to feel."

"But I loved him."

"I know you did."

Another silence fell between us. A large tear ran down the bridge of his nose to the tip, then dropped off onto his pillow. I shouldn't have been so surprised by his reaction, because people usually react to loss in ways that would surprise their closest friends. I didn't expect him not to be affected by the murder of the man he'd loved for so many years, but I hadn't foreseen that he'd fall so far apart. Being one of the most overtly masculine of our friends, I guess I thought he'd be more stoic. His reaction made me feel even more at a loss.

"So, Mother and I will go over to your place, and Peter will stay here."

"Okay."

Ryan rolled up into a sitting position with effort. He placed the doll gently on the bed with its head resting on the pillow. He looked at it for a second, then stood up. He wavered for a moment as if he'd just woken from a drugged sleep. He surveyed the room and walked over to the desk where his shorts lay folded with the precision of someone who'd just discovered the danger of creases. Like Mason would have done. All the while he looked like he was sleepwalking. He picked up the shorts and shook them out.

"What are you doing?" I asked.

"I should . . . I should help."

"No," I said, laying my hand gently on his arm. "No, we'll do it. You stay here and rest."

He stared at me blankly for a moment. "You'll need the keys."

"I have a set, remember?"

"Oh, yeah." He dropped the shorts back on the desk without refolding them.

I stood and returned the chair while Ryan sat back on the bed.

"You take it easy for as long as you want. You don't have to do anything. If you're hungry, Peter will fix something for you."

"Thanks," he replied absently.

I hesitated a moment, wanting to say something else to him when there was nothing else to say. Finally, I started for the door, but Ryan stopped me.

"Alex. I appreciate everything."

"It's no trouble."

He looked as if he wanted to say something else, but couldn't get the words out of his mouth. I think it was at that moment the impact of Mason's death hit me, at least in part, and I realized how death in general changes everything. The dead are gone, the living are forever changed. Ryan probably wouldn't always be as different as he seemed at this moment, but no matter how much he got past this, he'd still be different. We all would.

"Alex, I know Ryan wanted you to have his doll collection. . . ."

"Don't think about that right now."

"No, I mean, he told me that, and it's all right with me. It's just . . . there's not much left. You'll see. But you can have what's there." He glanced down at the Raggedy Ann doll. Its dumb smile beamed back at him. "But I want to keep this one."

Mother and I set out for Ryan's apartment, and I knew from her silence during the two-block walk that she was dreading what we might find there as much as I was. I fitted the key in the outer door, which opened smoothly. The door to Ryan's apartment was directly to the right at the bottom of a carpeted staircase that led to the second floor apartment. I unlocked the deadbolt, then twisted the other key in the doorknob and slid the door open.

The living room was exactly as it had been a few days ago when Peter and I were there for dinner. But I did have the eerie feeling that strangers had been here. We went through the living room and dining room, which was also untouched, and down the hallway to the doll room. The door stood open. I felt just like Tippi Hedren as she'd walked into the upstairs bedroom at the end of *The Birds.*

In the center of the room was a large pool of blood which looked sticky and not completely dry.

The room was scattered with the debris of broken dolls, almost all of which had been decapitated. Shards of china, bisque, and composition were strewn everywhere, as if someone had vented their frenzy by bashing in the dolls' heads. White dust was all over the place. I imagined half of it coming from the destruction of the dolls, the other half from dusting for fingerprints (though I have no idea whether or not that actually leaves dust).

I reached down to pick up a large, yellow-painted chunk of china.

"Careful," said Mother quickly, "don't cut yourself."

I rolled the piece between my fingers and recognized it after a moment as the porcelain scalp of the Dolly Madison doll. My hand trembled slightly as I remembered how recently and how lovingly Mason led me through his collection, and how impatient I'd been at the time. I would have let him describe each and every doll to me in mind-numbing detail if only I could have him back. My stomach sank at the sight of his Traviata dolls, all of which had been smashed to bits, including their delicate arms and legs. When I saw this it actually crossed my mind that I hoped whoever had killed Mason had done it before smashing the dolls, because the destruction of these treasures would surely have killed him in the end.

"Look at these," said mother, pausing by the elbow in the shelves.

Somewhat miraculously, some of the dolls had not been touched. The entire Barbie collection was unscathed, though Mason's Malibu Barbie had fallen onto the floor and was splattered with blood. And many of the character dolls, like Scarlett O'Hara and Dorothy from *The Wizard of Oz* had managed to escape harm. One by one we picked up some of the more intact figures from the floor.

"You know," I said as mother carefully placed a doll on a lower shelf, "some of these look like they were broken from falling rather than from being smashed.

"How do you mean?"

"Well, like this one," I said, showing her the Deanna Durbin doll, which now had a long, lightning-bolt–like crack running from the left side of her hairline down to the corner of her mouth. "It looks like she cracked when she fell, not like somebody tried to smash her." I continued to look at it for a moment, then sighed. "Mason would be heartbroken."

"Look at this," said Mother, picking up another one that had fallen just below the shelves. It was his prized Snow White figure, whose glaze had shattered, making it look as if she was covered with a tiny white spider web. "You know, I think you're right." She placed the figure gingerly on a shelf, trying not to cause any further damage. She looked back down at the floor and clucked her tongue.

"This is absolutely dreadful," she said with a frustrated sigh, "And I'm sure it didn't look good to the police."

"What do you mean?"

"Well, they can't possibly believe it was a robbery. If someone had broken in here to rob the place, they would have *taken* the dolls, not hurt them. Wouldn't any burglar worth his oats know that these were worth something?"

I shook my head. "I still can't believe that whoever did this knew Mason would be home, so it couldn't have been someone who knew them."

"But that's not the point," said Mother. "Having killed Mason, why smash things instead of stealing them? It must've taken as much time to do this as it would have to stuff them in a bag. And you know that's exactly what the police will be thinking. Lor', I can see—"

She glanced at me then turned away quickly, her cheeks reddening. She busied herself with picking up more debris.

"You can see what?" I pressed, having a pretty good idea already of what she was going to say. It had occurred to me, too.

She said with resignation, "I was just going to say I can see why the police would think that Ryan . . . or somebody else who knew Mason . . . had done this. Now that I see what's here, doesn't it look awfully . . . *personal* to you?"

"Actually, yes, it does. But I don't know anybody who would have done such a thing."

"Especially the way it was done. Look at how all of these heads are off. It looks like some mad thing had at them with a scythe." Mother's frown indicated both her distaste of the events and her perplexity.

"Maybe somebody was looking for something."

"Yes, but, darling, that brings me back to the question, why smash them?"

We pondered that one for a few seconds. My eyes were fixed on the pool of blood, but out of the corner I could see Mother wander to a shelf and gently examine a couple of the remaining figures. An idea came to me that almost made me gasp.

"Mother . . . maybe it wasn't a doll they were looking for."

"What do you mean?"

"Maybe they were looking for something inside one of the dolls. Like cocaine! You know, like in *Wait Until Dark*, where Audrey Hepburn has a doll full of cocaine, only she doesn't know it." I stopped and looked at Mother, who didn't reply. "What do you think?"

"I think I've been far too permissive with you."

"Why? What's wrong with that theory?"

"In the first place, I *hardly* think the drug cartels would need to hide drugs in dolls anymore—if they ever did. I think they just ship it nowadays. Like mangoes."

"And in the second place?"

Mother hesitated for a moment, her expression changing from amusement to sadness. "In the second place . . . I hardly think they could've gotten enough cocaine in one of these to do all this about, do you? Really, it's more likely that this was just a break-in. Darling, I know how hard it is to accept when something senseless happens to someone we love . . . but we do have to accept it."

My face went hot with anger, and I knew I had probably turned as red as the dress on the Scarlett O'Hara doll, but Mother continued to look at me steadily, her expression one of empathy. Still, I couldn't agree with her.

"The only problem with that is that you said yourself that this looks personal. I don't get any of it. Why would they have smashed half the dolls and not the rest?"

"Any number of reasons," said Mother thoughtfully, "the most logical of which would be that they were in the process of smashing them and got interrupted."

"By Mason," I said, nodding my head in agreement, "but having . . . dispatched him, I don't see why they didn't just go on with what they were doing, like you said."

"Panic, most likely. But I think you're missing something far more obvious."

"What's that?"

"Simply that they probably stopped because they found what they were looking for."

I raised my eyebrows at this.

It was at that moment that we were stopped by the sound of a woman's voice coming from the front of the apartment. As light and innocuous as the voice was, its unexpected arrival almost made my bones jump out of my skin.

"Ryan?" she called. "Mason?"

I peeked out the door and down the hallway. I could see the head of a woman with long, light blond hair craning into the apartment. I recognized her as Linda Brown, one of the girls who lived overhead.

"Hello!" I called as I headed down the hallway. Mother followed me.

A brief look of panic crossed Linda's face before she identified me as someone she knew.

"Hello?" she said, her questioning tone implying that she would be grateful for an explanation of my presence. She stepped into the apartment but left the door open. She was wearing a light purple silk dress that I would have mistaken for a slip if I'd seen it in a store, and her lips were painted to match the dress. Her eyelids were brushed very lightly with a contrasting shade of violet. She looked like a pastel popsicle.

"Hi," I said again, "You're Linda, right? I met you at Mason's Cinco de Mayo party last year, remember? I'm Alex."

"Of course I remember," she said, her tone still maintaining that question.

"This is my mother. We've stopped by to clean up a little."

Linda had been in the process of taking Mother's hand to shake it when she was stopped by what I'd said. Her face pivoted in my direction, she blinked slowly one time, and said, "Clean up a little?"

"Yes." Mother and I glanced at each other. "Uh, you don't know what happened, do you?"

"Happened?" She blinked again.

"Well," said Mother, "I'm sorry to have to tell you this, but Mason is dead."

Tears had begun to well up in Linda's eyes before Mother had even finished her sentence as if she kept them ready for bad news.

"Oh, God, no!" she said, and she clicked into the living room on a pair of impossibly high heels. She dropped onto the couch, her shoulders slumped. "I guess we've been expecting this, but no!" She shook her head and her hair cascaded attractively. I got the feeling it was a move she'd practiced for appropriate occasions, and had mistaken this for one of them.

Mother and I glanced at each other again. Mother rolled her eyes in a way that was surprisingly unsympathetic, but at least told me that she'd gotten the same impression I had. She sighed and sat down beside Linda.

"No, I'm afraid he didn't die of . . . He was sick, but that's not what killed him," mother explained.

"What?" said Linda, turning her face toward Mother. The little trails left by her tears glistened like Ingrid Bergman's at the end of *Casablanca.* I was beginning to feel unsympathetic myself, and had to remind myself that just because somebody is overly pretty and overly dramatic doesn't mean she can't be sincere.

Mother said as gently as she could, "Someone broke in here yesterday and killed him."

Linda blinked at mother then blinked at me. "But who . . . who would do something like that?"

"We don't know."

"Didn't you see the police here yesterday evening?" I asked.

She shook her head. "I met Ronnie for dinner after she got off work." If I remembered correctly, Ronnie was Linda's lover. "I didn't have to work myself yesterday. We went to a play with Ronnie's mother, then we stayed overnight at her house. We weren't back till the wee small hours." She looked back at mother and said, "Is that when it happened? Last night?"

"No, that's when the police were here. It apparently happened sometime during the day."

"The day . . ." said Linda. She looked for a moment as if she was concentrating hard, then her face lit up in a return to the panic that was there just briefly when she'd first seen me. Only this time it didn't pass. "During the day? When during the day?" she demanded.

"We don't know yet, but late in the afternoon, I suppose," I said.

She got up from the couch and headed for the door in the most halting fashion I've ever seen outside of a sitcom. She walked toward the door, then back toward us as if she was going to say something, then back toward the door a couple of times.

Mother finally said sharply, "What's the matter? Did you hear something or see something here yesterday?"

Linda wheeled around and faced Mother. "I didn't see anything!" She gasped, apparently having realized how she'd sounded. She placed her palms on her thighs as if she was trying to stop herself from trembling, then said more calmly, "I didn't hear anything, either."

This time she made it through the door, which she closed behind her.

"Well, that was entertaining," said Mother, rising from the couch.

"What do you make of it?"

She smiled. "The obvious, dear. Let's get this place cleaned up!"

We were at the apartment over three hours. Mother donned rubber gloves and scrubbed the floors till all signs of death had disappeared. For my part, I swept up all the remains of the dolls and bagged them. I found an empty box in the pantry and filled it with the dolls that had been spared, including the ones that were cracked but were in one piece. I was reluctant to take the dolls away, despite the fact that Mason had wanted me to have them, and despite the fact that Ryan had told me to take them. However, in the end I decided to take them because of the possibility that at that point, for Ryan, the dolls would just serve as a memory of how Mason had died. And there was also the possibility that the dolls had something to do with his death. Evidence. When mother was satisfied with the job we'd done, we went home, taking the box with us.

FOUR

We found Ryan and Peter in the living room watching Headline News on CNN. The look of abject grief that Ryan had worn since the murder had begun to give way to a more doe-in-the-headlights kind of blankness.

Mother greeted Ryan with a sympathetic "How're you doing, luvey?" then went on to explain that his apartment was all clean and tidy. She made it sound quite ordinary, as if we'd just gone over and picked up after a party. The British have an unerring habit of fighting trauma with a bravura show of normalcy. Whatever her intention, she served to distract him as I passed through the room with the box under my arm. I stashed the box beneath the staircase to the basement.

Later in the afternoon Mother requested Ryan's help in the kitchen, giving Peter and me a much needed break alone together, which we spent by going for a walk. The streets had the late-afternoon bustle of suited people heading home from work. Despite the traffic, Peter and I held hands as we walked, something that we and our brothers-and-sisters-under-the-skin are usually loath to do in public. But I didn't care. I was sad and more than a little scared: Losing somebody nearby always makes you afraid that you'll lose someone closer. I held Peter's hand more tightly. Neither of us spoke.

When we returned home we found Mother busily whipping up a bowl of trifle as she nattered away at Ryan. His expression had become even more vacant. He looked like he was slipping away, while Mother fought to keep him in the present with a steady stream of innocuous conversation.

All during dinner a million thoughts were buzzing around in my head like pesky gnats. Foremost was the idea that the police probably really would stick to Ryan as the most obvious suspect, and if that were the case it would be up to my little team of spies— namely my mother and my husband—to try to track down the real murderer.

When we were just about through with dinner, I decided there was no time like the present to start asking some questions— especially since the silence around the table was beginning to get on my nerves.

"Ryan, did anything happen since we saw you last?"

Peter looked up from his plate, and Mother shot an annoyed glance at me.

"Huh?" said Ryan dully, "What do you mean?"

"Well, I was just wondering . . . about Mason. You know that I've known him for a lot of years. I don't know of anyone who didn't like him."

Ryan looked down at his plate for a few seconds. "I guess we all have enemies."

This surprised me. "Did Mason?"

He looked up. "There were people who didn't like him. Like a couple of my old friends. You know how it is when you pair off, not everyone likes your spouse, or understands why you . . . But I don't think anybody hated him."

"I see. That's why I was wondering if anything out of the ordinary happened since you had us over."

Ryan twisted his baseball cap absently with his right hand. He looked as if he were trying to read a street sign through a fog.

"No. Nothing."

I was disappointed. I don't know what I expected, but I really did think that Ryan might unknowingly hold some clue to what had happened. Assuming, of course, that it wasn't the obvious (as Mother had suggested earlier) and someone had just broken in to rob the place and killed Mason in the process.

Mother and Peter unobtrusively cleared the dinner plates and Mother brought in a tray of small dessert bowls full of trifle, which she distributed amongst us, while I continued to question Ryan.

"What did you do all week?"

"I worked."

"What about Mason?"

Ryan shrugged. "He stayed home. He did the normal stuff. I don't know."

I glanced at Mother, and though her expression hadn't entirely lost that disapproving edge, it was now tinged with interest.

I said, "So nothing unusual happened since we were over for dinner?"

"No."

I let that lie there for a moment or two, then said, "Ryan, was there anything unusual about the dolls?"

His face relaxed for a second, as if he was glad to be talking about something that was so dear to Mason. "All the dolls were unusual. You know that."

"Yeah. I just wondered because it's so odd that the dolls were broken the way they were."

"It was a nasty thing to do!" he replied warmly, angry on Mason's behalf.

"I know. And it's the oddest thing about his murder." I didn't bother to add "besides his being eviscerated." Peter glanced at me for a moment as if he was afraid I would.

"Was there anything out of the ordinary about the new doll?"

Ryan stopped in the act of moving his dessert around with his spoon—he wasn't exactly eating anything—and raised his head slowly to look at me. "The new one?"

"Yeah—was there anything unusual about it?"

The was a flicker of something across his face. If I had to

guess, I'd say he'd just realized something that hadn't occurred to him before. Both Mother and Peter had stopped eating and were watching him, apparently as interested as I was.

"No, there was nothing strange about it."

"Are you sure?"

"Of course I'm sure," he replied, his tone a little testy. With an attempt at regaining his normal manner, he said, "There was nothing. Um, he *did* take it to Marshall to be appraised."

Marshall was Marshall Torkelson, a mutual acquaintance of ours who owned an antique store. Though the doll in question wasn't an antique, Marshall did know enough to offer an educated opinion on such things.

"To be appraised?" Peter asked. "He just bought it. He knew how much it was worth."

There was a slight pause during which Ryan stared at Peter. I got the feeling he was debating with himself how to answer. "Yes, he often did that. I don't know why."

"Where did he buy it?"

"While we were in Washington. At a store . . . a specialty store. A little shop on Wisconsin Avenue in Georgetown. Just dolls and dollhouses, that sort of thing." An abbreviated smile, both touching and rueful, lit the corners of his mouth. "The type of place Mason loved. Just like you'd imagine, he thought he'd died and gone to heaven."

The smile disappeared.

After a minute's silence, Ryan looked at me out of the corner of his eye. I could have sworn there was something cagey in his manner, but frankly, he was such a mess at the moment it would have been difficult to judge anything he did in normal terms.

"Was it broken?" Ryan asked.

"What?" said Peter, his forehead wrinkling.

"His new doll. Was it broken?"

I glanced at Peter, who seemed as perplexed by the question as I was. It occurred to me that having been the last one that Mason had purchased, it might have some special significance for Ryan. "I'm afraid so," I said. "It was pretty much smashed."

"Oh," he said sadly. At least, I thought it was sadly. After a moment he said, "Did you . . . clean all of them up . . . ? The dolls, I mean."

"Oh, yes, we did," said Mother.

"What did you do with them?"

This time Mother looked toward me. From her expression I gathered she thought this was a normal question from a grieving person.

"The majority of them were smashed," I explained. "We swept up all the debris and threw it away."

"Okay," he said. "That's good."

"The rest of them I brought here. I didn't know whether or not you wanted to see them. But they're here if you want them."

"No," he said, "I don't want them."

There was the slightest emphasis on the word *them*, which gave me the uncomfortable feeling that he wanted to keep the broken ones, though why he would do that was way beyond me.

We finished the rest of our desserts in silence. There didn't seem to be anything else to ask Ryan, and even if I could have thought of something, it didn't seem the time to push him any further. And we'd pretty much exhausted our ability for small talk. I was still puzzled by his reaction when I asked him about the doll. It gave me the uneasy feeling that Ryan, who was perhaps the most open person I'd known, was keeping something from us.

When he finished the last spoonful of trifle, he laid his spoon quietly on the table and sat for a few moments without saying anything. Finally, without looking up he said, "I think it's time for me to go home."

I glanced at Mother, and she looked honestly surprised. She said, "Oh, darling, you don't have to do that. Don't you think you'd be better off staying here a couple of days? You're more than welcome, and we've plenty of room."

He looked at her, his face completely devoid of expression. "No. It's time for me to go. I appreciate your . . . I appreciate everything you've done, but I want to be at home."

Mother looked as if she doubted the wisdom of his decision, but she didn't say anything. Ryan lingered with us for a while over the dinner table, making small talk about when he'd go back to work and other things that really don't seem to matter when someone has died, but there was a sense that he was anxious to go.

When he rose to leave, I went to the guest room and retrieved the Raggedy Ann doll for him, which he accepted with a slight blush. But his embarrassment couldn't hide the fact that he'd never part with the thing. Mother stopped him at the last minute and reminded him that he was forgetting their dog. We all looked down at the purebred mutt, which was looking up at Ryan with a slightly cocked head as if he would fully accept any command, but wished his co-master would make up his mind.

Ryan looked at Mother and said, "Would you mind keeping him for a few days . . . while I . . . while I . . ."

His voice trailed off. Mother said, "Of course we will. You just let me know when you want him back, and one of us will bring him over."

"Thanks," he said, with a curious look at the dog.

As he started down the walk, mother called after him, "I'll call you tomorrow to make sure you're all right!"

He waved to her limply as he disappeared down the street.

"Why on earth doesn't he want Muffin with him?" Mother asked incredulously as Peter closed the door.

"I don't know. Except that it really belonged to Mason. Maybe he doesn't want the reminder right now."

Mother bent down and stroked the dog's head. "I must say I would think he'd want his doggie with him."

It was the first glimmer that she, too, thought that Ryan was acting peculiar, even for someone in shock.

FIVE

S aturday morning Peter left at about nine-thirty for his job as premiere salesman at Farrahut's, the fey men's-clothing store. As for my own work, business was definitely not booming. Since getting involved as queer-in-residence at the CIA, I'm afraid my interest in graphic art had dwindled. This wasn't smart, because a freelance business can take a long time to build up and even longer to regain. And frankly, our CIA assignments were way too few and far between, not to mention trivial. But I still had a few steady clients for whom I designed brochures, booklets, and the like, and they pretty much provided the needed spending money. Given Mother's inheritance and her refusal to charge us rent, that was all I really needed.

So I was home when Mother called Ryan to check up on him. There was no answer.

"You don't think he would have gone to work today, do you?" I said as she hung up the receiver after her second attempt.

"There's no telling," she replied with a shrug. "Some people find it easier to work after a tragedy than to just sit home alone and brood on it."

"Was it my imagination," I said, "or did you get the impression that Ryan was hiding something, too?"

"Hiding something?"

"Last night at dinner, when I was asking him about this past week."

She thought a moment, then shook her head. "He wasn't normal, but that's to be expected. I don't know how much I'd make of it at this point."

"I don't mean that. I mean when I talked about the dolls. He seemed awfully interested in the last doll Mason bought."

Mother's lips drew up to one side, "You mean *you* were interested in it. You're projecting, darling."

I shook my head. "I don't think so. I think there was something odd about that doll."

"He told you straightaway that there wasn't."

"But then he asked about whether or not it was smashed."

"What's wrong with that?"

"And what we'd done with the rest of the dolls."

"He wanted to go home. He probably just wanted to make sure he wouldn't have to look at them."

I shook my head again and said, "But he asked about that doll specifically."

Mother sighed heavily and waved me off with a smile. "You've got dolls on the brain. I never should have let you play with them when you were little. Look what's happened!"

She tried to call Ryan a couple more times before Peter got home from work. After we'd had dinner, she gave me a sheepish grin and said, "I wonder if my boys would mind doing something for me."

"Sure," said Peter, always agreeable once he's been fed.

"I wonder if you'd go over and check on Ryan. He's got me just a little mithered with his not answering the phone."

"He probably just doesn't want to talk to anybody," I said.

"Perhaps, but would you mind?"

Neither Peter nor I could see what it would hurt to check on Ryan, so we walked down the street to his two-flat. The second-floor apartment was dark as far as we could see, while at least one of the living room lights was on in Ryan's apartment. As anyone from Chicago knows, the presence of a light doesn't necessarily signal the presence of an occupant. But I would have been surprised if he'd chosen to go out.

We went through the front door of the building to the door of his apartment. I pressed the bell and waited. There was no answer. After a minute or so I pressed the bell again, then knocked.

"Ryan?" I called through the closed door, "it's me and Peter. We just want to make sure you're all right."

Still no answer.

"Do you have your keys?" said Peter.

"I left them at home."

"Try the door."

I did what in the movies is described as a slow take and said, "No, *you* try the door. The last time I did that, I got in big trouble."

Peter hesitated for a moment then said, "Oh, honestly!" as if he was disgusted with our mutual timidity.

My stomach did an abrupt flip when Peter tried the door and found it was unlocked. Past personal experience and exposure to hundreds of horror movies over the years told me that this was a bad sign. Peter pushed the knob and the door slid open with a loud creak. Even in the dim light, we could see a trail of blood on the living room carpet.

"Call the police!" I whispered urgently to Peter. He started to turn away and I grabbed his arm. "No, call Frank!"

He glanced back into the living room, turned to look me squarely in the eye and said, "Alex, come away from here."

I pulled my arm away. "No! He might be—"

"Shhh!" Peter replied as harshly as he could without raising his voice. "We don't know what's happened and we don't know if anybody's still in there."

"I don't care!" I said anxiously. "It might not be too late! Even if somebody's there, I have to help Ryan!"

Peter hesitated a split second, just long enough for his anxiety over my welfare to be overcome by the knowledge that I was right, and ran off down the street to get help.

I looked into the apartment, craning my neck as far around the doorjamb as I possibly could while still maintaining an easy escape. The trail of blood stretched back down the hallway. Nobody was in sight. There were no sounds. I decided the best plan of attack was to make some noise from where I was.

"Ryan?" I called out loudly. I hoped that if an assailant was there this would startle him into making his escape by the back door. Though the first sight of blood had brought to mind the way Mason had been killed, it now occurred to me that it was possible that Ryan, in the state in which we'd last seen him, might have decided to take his own life. I called his name once more very loudly before venturing into the apartment.

I slowly followed the trail of blood across the Navajo rug in the living room and into the dining room, then down the hardwood floor of the hallway, all the while trying to keep close to the wall as if that would hide me from anyone who might come dodging out of another room. I realized with a sense of dread that the trail led back to Mason's doll room.

When I reached the doorway I paused for a moment. I was surprised to discover I'd been neglecting to breathe. I took a couple of deep breaths and exhaled as quietly as possible. The door was slightly ajar. I stayed plastered against the wall and pushed the door back with the fingers of my right hand.

Ryan was lying in the middle of the room. His stomach was cut open.

Peter returned, out of breath. By the look of him he'd expected to find me fighting off some unknown assassin. Instead he found me sitting on the couch, slumped forward with my head almost touching my knees. I wasn't trying to keep from throwing up or passing out (though both were possibilities), I just didn't feel like I had the energy to hold my head up any longer. I told him that Ryan was dead in the doll room, and he started to go back there but I took his hand and said "You don't want to see it" with enough intensity that Peter realized at once that he really *didn't* want to see it.

He said he'd tried Frank O'Neil's number at Area Headquarters, but had struck out. Unfortunately, Frank had gone off duty.

"I'm really sorry," he said with genuine remorse, "but I was so worried about you being back here alone that I went ahead and told them that something was wrong here, so they're sending someone over, but I don't know who. I told them this was where Mason was killed the day before yesterday. That seemed to pique their interest, especially since I was calling on Frank's private line."

"That's okay, there was no way around it."

Peter sat beside me and slipped an arm over my shoulder. "I called Frank at home when I got off the phone with his office."

"Is he coming?" I said, the anxiety in my voice almost making Peter start.

"Yeah. He said he'd be here as soon as he could, but someone from his department should be here first."

About five minutes had passed when we heard the steady clomp of the detective's arrival. We knew at once that mentioning Mason's murder had been a mistake. They sent Billings, since it had been his case. The front of his dark hair was matted to his forehead with sweat, and he was wearing the same suit he'd worn two days ago. It still hadn't been cleaned. Little drops of perspiration clung like dew to the area just above his eyebrows, and somehow made his eyes look beadier. He looked at me and folded his arms, his face smudged with a smug smile. I looked up at him, hoping my expression could show the amount of disdain I felt at the sight of him. I tossed a thumb in the direction of the doll room and said, "He's back there. It's Ryan Morton, Mason LaPere's husband."

A clump of nasty little wrinkles appeared on either side of Billings's nostrils at the word *husband*, but apparently he was at least worried enough about my knowing his commander that he didn't hazard to say anything. I suppose he wasn't worried about giving me a dirty look, since it would sound much more idiotic if I complained to his superior about his face. "Your detective was giving me dirty looks" sounds awfully silly coming out of a man in his mid-thirties, no matter how light he is in his loafers.

Billings turned away from Peter and me, dropped his hands into his pockets, and made off down the hallway. His partner went as far as the entrance to the hallway and stopped. I suppose there was some silent understanding between them that he was supposed to keep an eye on us.

Billings returned in a matter of seconds. He frowned his way through the dining room, shaking his head in disgust. By the time he reached us, the smug smile had reappeared. "Looks like somebody wants to make a salad out of you guys."

After going to his car to radio for whomever it is they call, Billings took a seat on the opposite side of the coffee table from us. His partner, whom Billings steadfastly refused to introduce by name, stood at the end of the couch looming over us. It was a childish tactic on their part, but recognizing it as such didn't make it any less effective.

"You guys seem to be showing up around a lot of dead bodies."

"We've been uncommonly unlucky this week," Peter replied, "but not as unlucky as our friends."

Billings looked at Peter as if he were something the detective had just scraped off his shoe. He leaned toward us, his eyes narrowing so that they looked like tiny black ball bearings stuck in the middle of crescents. "Let me tell you something . . ." He stopped just sort of saying "faggot." And that's not just my imagination: Any gay person can recognize when someone has stopped just short of calling him a faggot. Billings apparently knew that even in the midst of a threat, he couldn't cross that line. "Let me tell you something . . . buddy boys, you may think you're pretty damn cute but I'm here to tell you, you keep turning up with dead bodies and it ain't gonna matter if you know the king of France, you're gonna be in deep shit, you got that?"

I had to fight the urge to say something about the King of

France and Richard the Lionhearted, but I decided we'd pushed our luck enough already.

"Now, we got two dead . . . guys here, this guy and his . . . 'friend.' And you knew both of them. That looks pretty damn suspicious to me."

"They were a *couple*, detective," I said evenly, trying to control my anger. "Anyone who knew Mason knew Ryan."

"Uh huh," Billings replied.

Peter reached out and tapped the gold band on Billings's finger. The detective actually flinched. "This means you're married, doesn't it?"

"What's that got to do with anything?" said Billings, rubbing his finger as if he'd been burned.

Peter explained as if he were talking to a two year old. "Mason and Ryan were like you and your wife. If someone murdered you both, you could hardly suspect someone just because they knew the two of you."

"It's not the same thing!" Billings's cheeks went a nasty red.

"Yes it is."

The detective tried to bring himself under control, but it's extremely difficult to take deep breaths surreptitiously.

"Well, I wanna tell you something, buddy, I got two dead faggots—" Apparently he no longer cared how he chose his words.

"And the only good faggot is a dead faggot, isn't that right, detective?" I snapped.

"Alex . . ." said Peter in a cautioning tone. Although he found Billings as disgusting as I did, he didn't see any reason to further antagonize him.

Billings continued as if I hadn't said anything. "—the same kind of ritual killing, and the same two guys on the scene. I don't care who you are, that don't look good, does it?" He leaned towards us again. His face seemed to float in the air like a dew-speckled melon. "What is it, huh? Some kinda cult? Some church? Or you guys just decided to carve each other up?"

"How many pills does it take to get you to sleep at night?" I said.

Billings's stare grew colder, if that was possible. He sat back and folded his arms. "I don't give a flying fuck if the whole bunch of you kill yourselves off. World would be a better place. But not in my area. Come on, guys, you're making me have to look like I care."

"It's a living, isn't it?"

"Look," he said loudly, "I want to know what the hell the two of you were doing here tonight. How you came to be the ones that found the body."

"That's simple," I explained, trying my best not to appear rattled, "Ryan stayed with us after you charming people were through harassing him. Last night after dinner he said he wanted to come back home, which he did. My mother was worried about him because we couldn't get hold of him by phone today, so when *my husband*"—I stressed the term just to see Billings try to control himself some more—"got home from work, Mother asked us to come over here and check on Ryan. Which we did. And this is what we found."

Billings sat and stared at me, apparently hoping to make me uncomfortable. He didn't look like he believed me but I don't think he would have given me the satisfaction of looking like he thought I was telling him the truth even if he did. I figured he just liked making people squirm. I envisioned him as a little boy in ill-fitting rompers, pulling the wings off butterflies and frying worms under a magnifying glass.

"My mother will be glad to verify what I've just told you."

Billings rolled his eyes up at Peter and said, "Why didn't you tell us this friend of yours was dead when you called it in?"

"Because he didn't know," I continued. "We opened the door—"

"You opened the door?" Billings said as if he'd caught me up in something.

"Yes."

"Why?"

"Because he didn't answer the door and he hadn't answered the phone all day. We were worried about him."

"Why?"

"For Christ's sake!" I said loudly, losing my temper at last. "His lover was killed the day before yesterday! He was distraught over that, and as if that wasn't bad enough you people treated him like a criminal!"

"What's going on here?" The voice sounded unexpectedly from the doorway.

Billings shot a glance at the door, then looked back at us. His expression spoke volumes. He looked as if he thought we'd betrayed him and he hadn't expected us to, even though he obviously detested us.

Frank walked into the room, ignoring Billings, and I rose to meet him.

"Are you guys all right?"

"Yeah," I said, "Detective Billings and his significant other have been taking good care of us." Then, unable to hide my relief at the sight of him, my voice quavered as I added, "Ryan's been killed. Back there."

Frank went back to look at the scene. The evidence technicians arrived just as Frank rejoined us. Billings's silent partner showed them to the room.

"You were the one that discovered the body?" Frank asked.

"Yeah."

He was silent for a moment. He looked as if he was putting something together in his mind. Billings had risen when Frank entered the apartment, and he stood in front of his chair glowering at nobody in particular. Peter and I watched Frank.

After a minute or two, Frank exhaled and turned to me. "Your mother called me yesterday morning and asked if it was all right to clean up in here. She said she wanted to do that so the place would be ready for Ryan whenever he wanted to come back home."

"Yes, but we didn't expect him to come back so quickly."

He raised an eyebrow, as if what I'd said explained something to him. "Is that why you didn't do it?"

"Didn't do what?"

"Clean up."

I glanced at Peter, then back to Frank. "We did clean up."

Billings let out a snort that sounded like a pig. I would have been glad to wipe the smirk off his face with a lawn mower.

Frank said, half to Billings, "When Mason LaPere's body was found, wasn't there a lot of broken china?"

"Yes sir," said Billings. "Dolls. All over the place."

Frank looked back at me as if looking for some sort of explanation. The confusion was starting to irk me. "What?"

"They're still back there."

"What?"

"Bits of broken dolls. They're still back there. All over the floor."

I could feel the color leave my face. After a brief pause I ran down the hall to the doll room, my horror of the sight of Ryan's body was overcome by the disbelief of what I'd just heard.

There was Ryan's body. The evidence techs and the photographer were hovering over him. And there was something else: something I hadn't noticed because of my shock at finding Ryan dead.

Strewn about the floor were the remains of broken dolls.

SIX

At first I thought that just maybe these were the remnants of some other dolls (although I didn't know how that could be possible). I looked around the room, carefully trying to avert my eyes from the corpse of my friend, which wasn't entirely possible. The Raggedy Ann doll had been shredded and stained with blood and was lying a few inches from Ryan's outstretched fingers. I stepped carefully between the shards of broken china, tensing every time I heard an errant crunch beneath my shoes. After a couple of minutes, I saw something I recognized. I reached down and picked it up. It was the scalp of Dolly Madison. I was so stunned I barely noticed the lab technician who shepherded me out of the room.

"It's not possible," I said, stumbling on the edge of the rug in the dining room, still holding the piece of ceramic.

"I'd better get him a glass of water," said Peter. "Is that all right?"

Frank nodded to him. I slumped back onto the couch. "We cleaned it all up—yesterday—Mother and I. We got rid of all of them."

"You threw them all away?" said Billings sharply.

"Yes, we got rid of them all! If I remember correctly, you weren't interested in them. And we were given the okay to come in here and clean up."

"Maybe they had more dolls somewhere else," said Peter as he returned with the water. He handed me the glass and I took a drink from it.

"No," I said when I came up for air, "Look. This is a piece that was there when we cleaned."

"Are you sure?" said Frank.

"Of course I'm sure! Don't you think I'd recognize Dolly Madison's hair?"

Frank let that one go by. "What did you do with the ones you threw away?"

"We bagged them and put them out back in the garbage."

"Well, that would explain the garbage bag."

"What?"

"There is a soiled garbage bag in there. It would appear that somebody brought them back into the house."

"But why in the hell would they do that?" said Peter.

"That's something we'll have to find out," said Frank, then he turned to Billings and added, "Make sure you have all that debris swept up and delivered to the lab. We have to have that stuff gone over with a fine-toothed comb."

"Yes, sir," replied Billings, in a deferential tone that I'm sure caused him some pain. He turned on his heel and headed back to the doll room.

Frank sat down in the chair that Billings had vacated earlier. He looked down at the floor, then up at us. "Are you sure the two of you don't have any idea who did this?"

I blinked at him. "Of course we're sure."

"You have no idea who would want to kill these two guys?"

"None at all," said Peter, whose expression was a match for mine.

"Your mother told me on the phone yesterday that Ryan was staying with you."

"Yeah."

"Did he give you any indication . . . any hint that he might've known who killed his partner?"

"None at all," I said, shaking my head so vigorously my brain rattled. "He was as shocked as we were."

"More so," Peter added.

"He really didn't have a clue," I explained. "You've got to understand that Mason was as easygoing as they come. I don't think he had any enemies, except . . ."

"What?" said Frank.

"Oh, nothing," I replied with a wave of my hand, "just that I said something like that to Ryan and he said that there were people that didn't like Mason."

"But just like anybody else," Peter added quickly, "not anyone that disliked him enough to kill him."

Frank thought about this for a moment, rubbing the corners of his mouth with his index finger and thumb. He looked as if he didn't quite believe us.

"So he didn't say or do anything out of the ordinary while he stayed with you?"

"Only that he decided to come back here sooner than Mother thought he should. We were a little surprised by that, but Mother thought he was just anxious to try to get back to something like normal."

Frank continued to eye me with that same, doubtful look. Finally he released a heavy sigh and said, "Look guys, I know the two of you. I've known you for a long time, and I think that with rare exceptions you're pretty trustworthy."

The rare exception he was referring to was the first CIA case that we'd fallen into. We were put in the unfortunate position of having to deceive Frank about what was going on until the last minute, when we'd enlisted his aid. He'd assured us at the time that he understood why we'd had to keep him in the dark, but the fact that he mentioned it now proved to me that it had bothered him nonetheless.

"And?" said Peter.

"Well . . . I want to be sure that you're being straight with me," he said, then amended quickly, "I mean, that you're telling me everything you know about this."

I could feel the corners of my mouth drooping. I widened my eyes, trying to look as innocent and perplexed as I felt, and said, "Frank, we have no idea who's done this. Or why."

He let a beat go by before saying, "Because, you know, it wouldn't be the first time that you were involved in . . . investigating . . . something that included murder without my knowledge."

"Frank . . ."

He raised his palm to silence me. "But you have to understand that murder's murder, and when it happens in my area my people have to investigate, no matter what you or anyone else is doing. Because if you know anything about this, no matter how I feel about you or your mother, I may not be able to hold Billings back in pursuing it. I wouldn't do it, anyway."

I searched his face and could sense something of a smile behind his eyes. He was paying us back for keeping him in the dark on our first case (and possibly for having anything to do with the CIA, since law-enforcement officers are extremely proprietary about their little plots of ground), by playing a barely masked game of good-cop/bad-cop with us. My only consolation was that I was sure Billings didn't know he was in the game.

But there was something more in what Frank was proposing. I think he really did believe that we were involved in another . . . well, caper, for lack of a better word, that we weren't letting him in on. I would have been insulted that he didn't think I was telling him the truth, if only I hadn't lied to him so often.

I sighed deeply and said, "We don't have any idea what's going on here. This is *not* a 'case.' This doesn't have anything to do with the CIA or any part of the government. For Christ's sake! Don't you think we want you to find out who killed our friends? If we knew anything that would help you do that, we'd tell you."

"All right," he said with a hint of reluctance. Apparently he didn't want to let go of his doubts too quickly. "I believe you." There was a pause before he added, "But Alex, one thing you should know—when I checked the bedroom I found a suitcase on the bed, half-packed, with a pile of clothes next to it."

"What?"

"It looks like your friend was planning to run."

I was speechless for a minute, realizing what the implications of Ryan's departure would have meant to the police. Then I said, "If he was going to run, it was because he was in fear of his life."

Frank gave a nod. "Given what's happened to him, I'd say he had every reason to be."

On the way home I felt stunned and dazed. Billings and company had kept us so busy that I don't think it hit me until we were out of there that our friends had both been killed. My legs suddenly felt like rubber, and I was afraid they were going to go out from under me. I grabbed Peter's shoulder and he supported me.

"What is it?"

"I don't know. I guess I just realized that they're dead," I said.

"I know what you mean."

Peter wrapped his arms around me and held me for a few minutes. I took some deep breaths and then was ready to go on. He kept my hand in his, and it was one of those moments where in weakness I could feel myself drawing strength from my friend, lover, and companion in life. Energy seemed to pulsate from his hand into mine.

"God," I said when I finally detached myself, "I can't believe that he was going to run. He must've known why Mason was killed."

"Most likely."

"If he'd only told us what he knew," I said, tears starting to well up again, "maybe we could've helped him."

"Alex," Peter said soberly, "do you think . . . do you think this could have anything to do with Agent Nelson?"

Agent Lawrence Nelson is our "supervisor" on the occasional bits of work we do for the CIA.

"What?" I exclaimed, stopping in my tracks. "How could it have anything to do with the CIA?"

He shrugged. "Have you ever noticed that whenever someone gets killed around us, Agent Nelson manages to pop up?"

I put my hands on my hips. "I have a better question. Have you ever noticed how many people get killed around us? Christ, I'm beginning to feel like Jessica Fletcher. Pretty soon we won't have any friends left!"

Peter pursed his lips. His eyes were smiling. "You mean because they'll be afraid to be around us, or because there won't be any left?"

"Take your pick!" I said, and we both laughed uneasily. It was a little too close to the realm of possibility for comfort.

"No," I said as we resumed walking, "I would say if there's anything we can be sure about in this mess, its that for once it doesn't have anything to do with the government."

"Hmm," said Peter, "Not much consolation, is it?"

We went along in silence for a couple of minutes, then Peter said, "There's one thing, though, sweetheart. . . ."

"What?"

"Well, I think you forgot about it when Frank was talking to us, but you know we have that bag of dolls under the basement stairs."

"Oh my God, that's right!" I said, smacking my forehead. "But that doesn't matter. Even if I'd remembered I don't think I would have told them about it."

"Why? They're interested in the dolls now."

"I know, but despite what I told him, I'm too pissed off to help them. And besides, those dolls are all that's left of Mason's collection, and I'll be damned if I'll turn them over to those fat-handed idiots to paw over and pulverize!"

"How loquacious of you, lover," said Peter with a slight smile.

"Well, *you* knew about the dolls, why didn't you tell them about them?"

"I haven't gone all sentimental over them," he said quietly, "but I'm like you. I didn't want that Billings character manhandling Mason's prized possessions. Besides, Mason left them to you and they're yours to dispose of as you see fit."

I stopped again quite suddenly, grabbed Peter by the arm, and spun him around to face me. I shoved my arms through his, drawing him against my chest, and kissed him so hard I could almost feel myself draining into him. Our lips slid apart and we embraced.

"What was that for?" Peter whispered into my ear.

"I was just remembering how Ryan looked."

"It'll be hard to forget."

"No, I mean yesterday when I talked to him in the guest room. He looked so lost . . . He looked like he couldn't go on without Mason."

"Oh," said Peter, tightening his arms around me.

"I don't know what I'd do without you, and I don't want to find out. God, I love you!"

We held the embrace for a couple of minutes, then I pushed him gently to arm's length, waggled my right index finger at him, and said, "Don't you ever start collecting dolls. Look what it leads to!"

When we arrived home I opened the front door and was surprised by two heads swiveling in my direction from the couch in the living room. The two men sat across from Mother. They were dressed in identical gray suits. Though one had dark blond hair and the other light brown, they each had it combed back into submission. Both had very serious eyes and flat, unsmiling mouths. They looked so much alike they could have been brothers, but as they rose to greet me I realized this impression was more cultivated than natural. One was shorter than the other. They shared the mannerisms of men who came from the same school rather than the same womb.

"Mr. Hamilton and Mr. Dunn," said Mother by way of introduction.

Hamilton, the taller one, stretched out his hand to me and as I shook it I said, "Selling *The Watchtower*?"

"No," he replied with a singular lack of humor. He slipped a folder from his pocket and flashed it at me. "State Department."

"State Department? What are—"

"Um, darling," said Mother, judiciously cutting me off, "I was just about to make us some tea. Would you like to help me?"

"Tea won't be necessary, Mrs. Reynolds. We don't need anything, and hopefully we won't be staying long," Hamilton said quickly. The way his eyes shifted to one side made it seem as if he thought we were trying to pull something.

"It's no trouble at all!" Mother replied airily as she headed for the kitchen, "I was just about to make some for my boys! Entertain them, will you Peter?"

"You never should have mentioned Nelson," I whispered to Peter before following Mother.

Mother quickly busied herself with making the tea as if it was a necessary annoyance. "Pull some biscuits out of that jar and put them on a plate," she commanded, "We don't have much time."

As I complied, I said, "Mother, Ryan's dead. He's been murdered, just like Mason."

"I know."

My eyes widened. "How's that possible?"

She cocked her head in the direction of the living room. "They told me. They seemed to know all about it already. And they told me the two of you were all right."

"Did they tell you he was killed in the same way Mason was?"

"Good God, no!"

"Yeah, so we were wrong about one thing: Whatever this murderer was looking for when he killed Mason, he didn't find it, because he came back . . . and so did the dolls."

"What?" she said incredulously.

"I'll tell you about it later."

Mother thought for a minute, then made a tsking noise. "I don't like these people showing up like this. Especially with them knowing about Ryan almost before it's happened. I mean, they say they're with the State Department . . ."

"You have some doubt?"

"Don't you think if they wanted to contact us, they'd do it through Larry Nelson?"

"Why? The State Department isn't the CIA, so they probably don't even know we're with the agency. You know from our rather lurid past experience that the right hand doesn't know what the left hand is doing in our government."

"I suppose that's true," said Mother, her face relaxing just a bit. "What does the State Department do, anyway?"

"How on earth should I know?"

"You're an American, aren't you?"

"Good Lord, what does that have to do with anything? You had to learn more about America than I did when you got your citizenship."

"I suppose."

"Did you tell them we're with the CIA?" I asked.

"Of course not!" Mother replied indignantly. "I didn't know—I still don't know—what they're here for, so I kept my mouth shut. When they started asking questions, I realized they didn't know who we were."

"Asking questions?" I said, putting the cookie jar back on the counter. "About what?"

Mother sighed. "I'm not quite sure, but it has something to do with Mason, since all they've done so far is ask about him. I have a feeling Mason was in some sort of trouble."

"Good guess, seeing as how he's been killed."

She grimaced at me but chose to go on without comment. "But they got here just before you did, so your guess is as good as mine."

The kettle had begun to whistle. Mother lifted it from the stove and poured it into the ceramic pot that sat on our serving tray surrounded by matching mugs. I was always glad that Mother didn't go for the typical British teacups, but instead insisted on mugs for a "proper lot" of tea.

"I suppose we'll find out what they want," she said as she swept through the kitchen door. I followed closely with the plate of cookies and laid them on the coffee table in front of the G-men.

"Here we go," said Mother, "nice and hot. Now, you were saying?"

Mother poured out as the conversation continued. Neither of the agents took any interest in the mugs placed before them. In fact, they took too little interest in the mugs, as if they didn't want to touch anything. Hamilton looked at Mother for a split second as if he would've liked to chastise her for scurrying out of the room, and cleared his throat.

"We understand that the three of you were familiar with Mason LaPere."

"He was a friend of ours, if that's what you mean." I didn't mean to sound quite so snappish, but government agents have a tendency to phrase things in a way that makes the simplest statement sound like an accusation.

"Exactly how did you come to understand that?" Peter asked.

Hamilton flashed an enigmatic smile as he answered, which led me to believe he was anxious for us to understand he didn't need to answer our questions.

"In checking into Mr. LaPere's background we found that he used you, Mr. Reynolds, as a reference on some employment applications."

"I didn't know Mason had ever applied for work with the government," I said.

"I didn't say he had," Hamilton replied.

Mother, Peter, and I glanced at each other. The gravity of this statement sunk in.

"Why would you be looking into Mason's background, Mr. Hamilton?" said Peter with an edge in his voice. "Just for sport?"

"And what possible difference could his background mean now?" asked Mother. "He's dead, and so's his husband."

Hamilton sat back as Mr. Dunn, who had so far been his silent partner, leaned forward. The move looked choreographed.

"As to looking into his background, we were interested in finding out what kind of American he is . . . was."

"What *kind* of American?" I said. "He was a *gay* American."

Dunn looked at me as if I needed to be spanked. "We know

66

that. Perhaps I should have been more clear. I meant we wanted to know whether or not he was a patriot."

"I don't know what you mean by that," said Peter hotly. "From the way the government treats us, you would think we weren't citizens. How patriotic can you be to that?"

"Peter . . ." said Mother quietly. She sounded not as if she was warning him, but as if she didn't feel this was the time or place. She also sounded as if she agreed with him. Mother can put an awful lot of meaning into one word.

"Mason loved this country," I said firmly, "no matter how the country may have felt about him. Now what's this all about? Mason's dead. I would think you could leave him alone now."

Dunn sat back just as Hamilton lurched forward. They were beginning to remind me of a pair of scissors.

"His death, and the death of his partner, are what brings us to you. It's believed that on Mr. LaPere's recent trip to the nation's capital—"

"You know about that?" I cut in incredulously.

Hamilton looked at me a second before answering. "Circumstances have brought that to our attention, yes."

"What circumstances?"

"If you please," said Hamilton with marked patience, "it's believed that on Mr. LaPere's recent trip to the nation's capital, he may have come into possession of . . . something of importance to the government."

I could feel the color drain from my face. "Like what? I hope you're not going to say microfilm." I tried to sound sarcastic, though inwardly I was really hoping it wasn't microfilm because we'd once gotten involved in something like that and it nearly cost us our lives.

"Nothing quite so prosaic, I'm afraid," said Hamilton with an indulgent smile. "Just an object."

"Well, what was it?" Mother asked. She was beginning to lose her patience with these guys.

"Exactly what it is doesn't matter," he replied flatly. "What we want to know is whether or not Mr. LaPere said anything to you about . . . having such an object or what he might have done with it."

"Well, now, there's a difficulty," I said, "because without knowing what you're looking for, how're we supposed to know whether or not Mason mentioned it?"

"You'd know."

Out of the corner of my eye I could see Mother's eyebrows slide upward.

Dunn leaned forward, but this time Hamilton stayed in place. I wondered if I had made him forget his steps.

"Can we take it that you're unwilling to cooperate?"

"You can take no such thing!" said Mother indignantly, "We have cooperated with the government on several occasions. The only thing you can take is that we don't know what you're talking about."

Hamilton said, "Mr. LaPere never mentioned finding or having anything unusual?"

"Nothing," I replied with finality. "Why didn't you ask Mason about this before he got killed?"

Dunn made a little noise in his throat, as if he was clearing it but only halfway. "Unfortunately we didn't know about Mr. LaPere until it was too late. By the time we found out about him, he and his friend had been murdered."

"You found that out rather quickly, didn't you?" said Mother.

"Yes," Hamilton replied without explanation.

"Well, whatever it is you're looking for must be over in their apartment."

Dunn cleared the rest of his throat. "We have reason to believe that it wasn't in their possession when they were murdered."

Mother's eyebrows merged with her hairline. Peter looked extremely displeased and I was just confused. Suddenly Peter said, "Is that why you're here? You think we have whatever it is you're looking for?"

Hamilton's smile was becoming downright scary. "You were friends of theirs. We thought it might be a possibility."

"I hate to disappoint you," said Mother, "but if they didn't discuss it with us they surely didn't give it to us, whatever it may be."

The agents looked each of us in the eye in turn, then rose as one.

"We thank you for your cooperation," said Hamilton, drawing out the last word significantly. He took a business card from his wallet and handed it to Mother. "If you happen to . . . remember anything, would you please give us a call?"

I glanced at the card over Mother's shoulder. It was a number in Washington, DC.

"I assure you, Mr. Hamilton, that we won't be calling because we have nothing to remember."

"As you say," Hamilton said cryptically. With that, he and his partner left.

Mother closed the door behind them, wheeled around, and looked me straight in the eye.

"All right, what have you done?"

I glanced from her to Peter and back again. "*Me?* I haven't done anything! What are you talking about?"

"Oh, I don't know, darling," she said, dripping with irony, "but when the State Department ends up in our living room I just can't help thinking that you have something to do with it!"

"How can you say that?"

She pursed her lips at me as she continued, counting the events off on her fingers, "You go to a bar and we end up in the middle of the CIA. You watch a dirty movie and we end up at—"

"All right, all right," I said, "there's no need to dredge up the past. My God, first the police, then the State Department, and now you. I don't know any more about this than you do."

She folded her arms across her breasts and raised her right eyebrow at me.

"I swear!" I added defensively.

"Really, Jean, he's telling the truth," said Peter. "We're in the dark . . . for the most part."

Mother turned her questioning gaze on him.

"Well . . . we know a little more than the police, and I think we know what the State Department didn't want to tell us."

"And what would that be?"

"It was something to do with the dolls," I said. "Remember when we were cleaning up yesterday? We were talking about how the murder might have had something to do with the dolls."

Peter nodded. "Now the police are interested in them."

"Yes," I said, "it's what I started to tell you in the kitchen. The dolls came back."

She expelled a hot breath. "What kind of daft nonsense is that?"

"It's true! We found Ryan lying there dead—in the doll room—and the remains of the dolls were scattered all around."

"But we threw them out!"

"Somebody brought them back in. Apparently the murderer."

Mother's expression softened into a confused daze. She put her fingers to her temples and dropped down onto the couch. "Oh, Lor', I don't believe it."

"It's true, Jean," said Peter. "They were all there—the ones that had been destroyed before. Garbage bag and all."

"But that doesn't make any sense."

"I know," I said, nodding my head.

"No, I mean that the murderer would have brought them back in the house. First of all he—or she—wouldn't have known where they were. Why on earth would they have looked out back in the garbage? And second, even if they found them there, why would they bring them in the house? Why not just take them away? No, I think it's much more likely that *Ryan* fetched them back into the house."

"Why would he do that?" I said.

"Probably because he knew what it was Mason discovered in one of them," Peter explained. "You know Mason never would have kept it a secret from Ryan. Ryan must've wanted to look for it himself."

"And the killer returned," I said, completing the thought.

"Exactly," said Mother, "but why? I mean, the first time they were there, if they hadn't found what they were looking for and they'd killed Mason and had him out of the way, why didn't they just go on looking for whatever it is? Why didn't they break up the rest of the dolls or take them away?"

After she said this we fell silent for a moment. Muffin chose that moment to come trundling down the stairs. When he saw Mother was seated, he made a beeline for her, leapt up on the couch, and sat down beside her. She petted his head for a moment. Then suddenly Mother's eyes widened and she rose from the couch. Muffin sat up expectantly.

"The rest of the dolls! Oh my Lord, we have the rest of the dolls!"

"I know that."

"But don't you see what danger we're in? We've got to get rid of them!"

"No," I said, trying to sound more calm than I felt, "we've got to find what's hidden in one of them."

"Alex, those fellows from the State Department wanted to know if Mason had given you anything. You can't withhold evidence from them."

Peter shrugged. "Jean, we've withheld evidence from the CIA and the FBI. What's one more department?"

"I'm not withholding it from the feds," I protested, "I'm withholding it from the police."

Mother blinked at me.

"There's a difference."

"Difference or not, I'll not have those things here with people getting killed over them! We have to turn them over to somebody."

"I won't give them to the police. Not after the way they treated us."

"Frank isn't—"

"Frank's not the one I'm worried about . . . even though I wasn't exactly pleased with him tonight, either. He thinks we're holding out on him."

"Well, you are!"

"Not intentionally! When they were questioning us, I just

didn't think about the dolls. But either way, right now I'm in no mood to give them to them."

"Well, then, the State Department."

"I'm not turning them over to strangers, either. What I'm going to do is . . . Tomorrow morning I'm going to call Nelson and make sure there really is an investigation going on."

"If it's a State Department matter, he may not know about it," said Peter.

"But he'll be able to find out about it. And he can check up on those two junior G-men that were just here. I'd hate to think I'm getting paranoid, but I'm not going to accept that they work for the State Department just because they say they do. If Nelson finds out they're all right, *then* we'll hand the dolls over."

"Assuming, of course, that we can trust Nelson," said Peter in the tone people use when they're discussing the low quality of cafeteria food: more out of a matter of principle than belief.

"But first I think we should do a little investigating on our own, starting with the dolls."

Mother shrugged and looked down at the dog. The left corner of her mouth went down as if she was taking pity on the poor animal. "And you, little darling, it looks like you're our doggie now."

"Then there's one thing we have to do before we do anything else," I said.

"What's that?"

"Change his name!"

SEVEN

We spent the remainder of our waking hours practicing vivisection on the bag full of dolls. Our progress was greatly hampered by not knowing what the hell we were looking for. On the dolls that sported clothes we stripped off the gowns and underthings (something I was only able to do after Mother assured me that the dolls would not be anatomically correct), and searched the hems and linings and everywhere else we thought an object might be hidden. We found nothing. Then we carefully took the heads and limbs off the dolls and examined their interiors. We also peered inside the torsos and felt around their outsides for suspicious lumps.

"I feel like I'm performing a breast examination," said Mother at one point.

Three hours later we replaced the bag and went to bed, sadder and no wiser.

I sat on the edge of the bed and watched Peter strip down to his khaki shorts. He's one of those rare men who look beautiful both in and out of their clothes. We climbed into bed, wrapped our arms around each other, and tried to get to sleep. It turned out to be very difficult.

My mind was filled with that forlorn look Ryan had worn at the loss of Mason. I laid my arm across Peter's chest, and as I felt the familiar warmth a wave of fear washed over me at the idea of what it would be like if he wasn't there any more.

"Honey?" I whispered "are you awake?"

"Yeah."

"I was just thinking . . ."

"I know."

I propped myself up on my elbow. "How do you know?"

"Because I was thinking the same thing."

"Oh, really?" I said, smiling in the darkness. "And how do you know that you were thinking the same thing I was?"

He reached over and pushed the hair back off my forehead. "I just know." He sighed deeply. "We should try not to think about it."

"How?"

"By trying not to think at all." As he said this he drew my face to his and our lips came together. I met the familiar wet roughness of his tongue, and I realized how smart my husband was. I'd already forgotten what I'd been thinking about. There's something about losing yourself in someone you've given your life to that makes you realize you're never really lost.

As we continued to kiss, Peter's left hand trailed slowly down my chest and stomach, and into my shorts. After seven years together, I'm still excited just by his touch. Everything after that is a blur of hair, sweat, and tossed sheets.

The next morning I called Nelson who, true to form, was answering his number even though it was Saturday. I suppose CIA agents are supposed to give the impression of omnipresence. I gave him part of the story (leaving out the part about us having the remaining dolls), and asked him if he'd check out Hamilton and Dunn.

Nelson sounded disinterested but he sounds that way even when being shot at, so I didn't attach too much importance to it. He also doesn't often offer compliments, so I was surprised when he said, "It was a good idea for you to call."

"Really?"

"Yes. You should always check things like this out first. One question. What are you checking it out for?"

"What?" I said stupidly, fearing that as usual I'd made a mistake somewhere.

"If you don't have anything to give or tell these people, why are you checking them out?"

"Oh . . . well, just because they came here to our house, and we want to make sure they're on the up and up, you know?"

It sounded lame even to me. Nelson paused before he said, "You realize of course that like any other citizen you are required to cooperate in a State Department investigation."

"If it really is one," I said, hoping to distract him.

There was another pause before he added, "Of course." There was a smile in his voice. "I'll get back to you, but it may take some time."

I thanked him and hung up. In the course of our brief and inauspicious association, I've always found it disarming that Nelson seems to know when I'm not being completely candid with him. It doesn't so much make me feel guilty as it makes me feel silly.

Peter and I decided that with two people dead we wouldn't wait to hear back from Nelson before we started investigating. But before we headed out, we carried out the task I had set the night before: We renamed the dog. I decided to call him Duffy, because it sounded enough like his former name that I was pretty sure he'd respond to it, and because though not overly macho it was at least masculine enough to make the poor animal sound like he had balls (at least that he was born with them—he was no longer carrying them around). Peter and Mother had allowed me to choose the name out of the misplaced notion that it would help me bond with the animal. He should live so long.

That ceremony complete, Peter and I went to work. For once it was easy for us to know where to start, because in addition to having the rest of the dolls, we knew one other thing that the police didn't: Mason had taken his newest doll to be appraised. We set out for *The Old and the Beautiful*, the antiques shop owned and operated by Marshall Torkelson, the aging queen to whom Mason had brought his new doll for appraisal. Mother decided to stay home because she thought we might get further with Marshall on our own, and because she thought it only right and proper that she stay with the dog on his first day as an official member of our family. I wasn't kidding about the British attitude toward dogs.

Peter and I took the El up to Belmont and walked over to Lincoln, having decided not to drive because parking can be a challenge in that particular area. Marshall's shop was about two blocks south in one of those old storefronts with a recessed entrance across which a huge metal gate is drawn at closing.

Despite the large windows in front, the store is so crammed with goods that the interior is perpetually dark. It always reminds me of *The Old Curiosity Shop*, though Marshall is more like Miss Haversham than Quilp. He's a cadaverous, diminutive man who, when I met him, had a frosting of white hair that has become a snowdrift. His cheeks are sunken and his nose falls just short of a beak. His hands are so slender that a mutual friend once remarked that if one ever allowed Marshall to insert a finger into one's orifice, one wouldn't feel a thing. I shuddered at the thought. Marshall wears expensive Italian suits to work, presumably to demonstrate that despite the jumble within the shop's walls, the goods and the proprietor are quality merchandise. There were no customers in the shop when we entered.

"Well, well," said Marshall in his reedy voice. "Look who we have here! How are you, my pets, and how is Mother?"

He gave us each a discreet peck on the cheek, and I tried not to wince. Marshall has very thin lips that he puckers like a goldfish when he approaches.

"Mother is fine," I said, "and so are we."

"Lovely, lovely. You boys are just in time. I have, of late, taken in the most *beautiful* oaken sideboard you'd ever hope to see, and

I'm sure it would be just the thing for that living room of yours."

Peter and I glanced at each other. Though we've known Marshall many years, I can't remember him ever being in our home, and apparently neither could my husband. And we already had a sideboard.

"Sorry," said Peter, "but actually we didn't come to shop today."

"Oh? Then to what do I owe the honor of this visit? Surely you didn't come just to visit poor little me?"

"Um, no," Peter continued, "we came to talk to you because of what happened to Mason LaPere."

"Oh, dear, dear Mason," said Marshall. He clasped his hands just below his chest. I half expected sparks to fly as his bony knuckles clacked against each other. "A tragedy. Surely a tragedy."

"Yes, it is. And even worse now."

"What do you mean?" Marshall's eyes had widened, his hands going to his cheeks. He looked like a gay leprechaun posing for Munch's *The Scream*.

Peter sighed. "I'm afraid Ryan's been killed, too."

"Oh, no!" cried Marshall. "Oh, my dear! Oh, my *dear!*"

Marshall's head rolled backward and he flung a hand out in my direction. I caught it as Peter slipped a hand under Marshall's other arm. He was trembling all over, but even though we were supporting him, he seemed to be leading us as he staggered toward a Victorian fainting couch and allowed himself to be lowered onto it. He passed the back of his hand over his forehead and rolled his sunken eyes in my direction.

"I don't . . . Do you think . . . I have some tea on back there." He waved a limp hand toward the back of the shop.

"Of course," said Peter, and went to retrieve some.

"Oh, my dear," said Marshall again, dropping his hands to his sides and vacantly staring straight ahead, "this is simply terrible! Do you think . . . You don't think someone's out to get us all, do you?"

"All homosexuals? Oh, no, I'm sure that's not it," I said. "I mean, I don't think it was random, I think someone killed Mason and Ryan in particular . . . for a reason. A reason that the police can't seem to find at the moment."

"They can't?" said Marshall, sparing enough energy to force a wry smile, *"That's* a surprise."

"It's early days yet."

"My dear, dear boy," he said with a condescending smack of his lips, "it's always been my experience that the police are blind, deaf, and dumb when it comes to crimes against the daintier males of the species."

I didn't respond. I don't know many men, gay or straight, who could be considered dainty. Ryan certainly wasn't. Mason either, for that matter. Except for the dolls.

Peter arrived with a teacup and saucer, both of which looked as delicate as their owner. He handed them to Marshall, who quickly took a sip then replaced the cup on the saucer, which he continued to hold very carefully. The tea seemed to calm him a bit.

"I'm so sorry to give way like that, but it's such a shock! Those two beautiful boys! Why, they were like my own . . . like my own . . ."

"Sons?" I offered.

He sniffed and glanced at me from the corner of his eye, which had narrowed slightly. "Brothers. They were like my own brothers. Oh, God, that they should come to this!" He took another sip of tea.

"We hate to give you the news like this," said Peter, "but it couldn't be helped."

"I had to know sometime," Marshall said with another sniff. "It was very kind of you to take the time . . ."

"Uh, that's not exactly why we came," I said.

Marshall's eyebrows slid upward into two perfectly rounded crescents that looked out of place on his angular face.

I continued. "Ryan told us the other day that Mason had brought his new doll to you."

Marshall smiled in remembrance. "Oh, yes, he loved those dolls, and he had quite a lovely collection."

"Yes, well, we were wondering if there was anything unusual about the doll."

He blinked, then said primly, "For what reason? Did he leave them to you?"

I glanced at Peter. "Well, as a matter of fact he did, but—"

"My God," Marshall interrupted with a dramatic wheeze, "they're not even cold in their graves yet and already the vultures are tearing over the spoils."

I heaved a sigh along with a silent prayer for patience. "No, Marshall . . . whether or not the dolls were left to me is a very moot point. Most of the dolls were destroyed—"

"My God!" he said again, sitting up, "Don't say that!" What little color there had been drained from his face, leaving the indentations in his cheeks looking like two triangular smudges. The cup and saucer rattled in his hand. "That collection was fabulous! Say it isn't true!"

"I'm afraid it is. Whoever killed Mason smashed most of the dolls, for whatever reason. Now, one of the last things that Ryan told us was that Mason had just brought his newest doll to you for your opinion."

"Yes . . . yes he did. It was a truly lovely piece. Not worth any more than Mason paid for it, mind you, but the workmanship was lovely. The type of thing that I predicted would have increased in value manyfold over the passing years. Not that poor Mason would've seen that happen, or that he even cared. You understand that he just asked me my opinion as a matter of course. He didn't really need it. Like any collector, he'd developed an eye of his own. He could tell the fruit from the dross. But he wanted a second opinion."

The fruit from the dross? I thought to myself.

"So there was nothing unusual about it?" asked Peter.

"Not in the least," Marshall replied. He took a couple more sips of tea and laid the cup and saucer on a kidney-shaped coffee table that must have hailed from the fifties. He then added innocuously, "Of course, Mason was rather odd about it."

"How so?" Peter asked.

"Oh, nothing really. It's just that he didn't seem to be as interested as usual in whether or not he'd gotten a good price."

"Really?"

Marshall nodded. "Yes, he seemed much more interested in the origins of the piece."

"That was unusual?"

"Oh yes, oh yes, he was usually very interested in whether or not he'd gotten a good price." Marshall leaned toward us confidentially. "Like most of us boys, he very much liked it when he found he'd gotten a bargain. And he did most of the time. He was a very shrewd collector."

"But he didn't care about the price?"

"No, he was much more interested in where it came from."

"Where was that?"

"Thailand," Marshall said with finality. "I would stake my reputation on it."

"Is there anything unusual about that?" Peter asked.

"Not in the least," Marshall replied airily, "but Mason certainly seemed to find it intriguing. He asked me all I knew about Thailand, but of course that's next to nothing. I've never been there. And what do I know of third-world countries?"

Actually, until he said that I never even thought of Thailand as a third-world country.

"I never go anyplace where one can't be sure of the plumbing," Marshall added. He paused and passed a desiccated hand across his forehead as if the effort of relating this story had almost been too much for him. It completed the picture of a fading Victorian heroine. "Dear me," he said with a sigh.

"You looked the doll over?" I asked after a pause.

"Um-hm."

"And you're *sure* there was nothing different about it?"

"Not outside of it being particularly exquisite, given where it was made. We tend to think of those people, you know, as being a bit on the unclean side."

"*We* do?" I said, curling my lips.

Peter shot me a warning glance, then said, "So he just showed you the doll. He didn't show you . . . anything else."

Marshall blinked his dewy eyes at us. "No, of course not. He only collected dolls."

I said, "We just thought he might have come across something else and showed it to you."

"Like what?"

"We don't know."

Marshall looked from me to Peter, and then back to me. He barely moved his head, although I half expected his neck to creak from the little movement he did use.

"Now, boys, what are you up to?"

"What do you mean?"

He tapped the tips of his fingers together. I swear I saw a spark that time. "Dropping in here like this, these questions. This is very unlike you."

It was more like us than Marshall would ever know, as long as our affiliation with the government remained a secret.

"Well, to tell you the truth," said Peter, "Alex and I feel the same way about the police as you do. They're a bunch of idiots, especially when it comes to crimes against the gay community. So we thought we'd do a little nosing around on our own."

Once again I was a little taken aback at how quickly my husband can come up with stuff like that. It's a talent he shares with my mother, and I find it even more disarming when she does it. But it had the desired effect. Marshall beamed at us like a proud funny-uncle and said, "That's wonderful! That's wonderful! My dear boys are being sleuths in arms. And have you gotten anywhere yet?"

"No, we've just started," said Peter, "and please don't tell anyone we're doing it. We wouldn't want it to get around. I might keep people from talking to us."

"Oh, no, no, no," Marshall replied, putting his skeletal index finger to his lips. He looked like he enjoyed being part of a conspiracy. "I won't breathe a word."

"Thanks," I intoned. Peter shot me a glance that I don't care to record.

"Now, you're sure that Mason only showed you the doll. He didn't ask you about anything else," Peter said to Marshall.

"Oh yes, I'm sure," Marshall nodded eagerly. "If he had something else of value, he didn't show it to me."

The moment we were in the door Mother told us that Margaret LaPere, Mason's mother, had called to tell us that they had planned to have a memorial service for Mason on Monday evening, but given current events they had expanded it to include Ryan. Mother had assured her that the three of us would be there. We filled her in on what Marshall Torkelson had to say.

"We're no farther along," I said. "Whatever Mason found in the doll, he didn't show it to Marshall. All he did was ask a lot of questions about Thailand. I was really hoping he had gone to Marshall to get an appraisal of what he'd found."

"Maybe it was something he couldn't readily have appraised," Mother offered. "Like a microdot or something."

"A microdot?" I said incredulously.

Mother pursed her lips at me. "We *have* found sillier things in our short, lamented career with the CIA, darling."

I was trying to get past the absurdity of having one's mother say something like that when Peter said, "I don't think so, Jean. I mean, would Mason have recognized something like that? And how would he have found it?"

"Yeah," I added, "I would think that with the type of questions he was asking, he had to have some idea that what he found was valuable."

"I suppose you're right," Mother said with a frown.

We were silent for a few moments, each of us lost in our own thoughts.

"You know," said Mother at last, "none of this makes me feel any too easy about having the rest of those dolls here."

"Come on, Mother. Whoever killed Mason and Ryan must have found what they were looking for. We dismembered what was left of them last night and didn't find a damn thing."

"Yes, darling, but we didn't know what we were looking for.

It could be very, very small for all we know."

I shook my head. "They must have gotten it when they came back and killed Ryan."

Peter said, "The State Department seems to think it's still missing."

"Well, they can't possibly know whether or not the killer got what he was looking for. Unless, of course, they're involved somehow. But I don't think that's likely."

"Oh yeah," said Peter wryly, folding his arms across his chest, "We all know that the government would never have anything to do with murderers."

"Unless . . ." I said, thinking out loud at first. But then an idea came to me. "Oh God, I'm an idiot! Of course!"

"What?" Peter and Mother said simultaneously.

"Whatever Mason found, he didn't leave it in the doll! He hid it somewhere else."

"But where?" said Mother. "The police are sure to have gone over the apartment, and we've gone over what was left of the dolls. Nobody found anything."

The three of us exchanged frustrated glances. We were stymied and we knew it, but it was Mother who finally voiced it.

"Well, we're at a standstill, then. The killer may or may not have found what they were looking for when they came back, but whoever does have it, it's not us, so there's an end to it."

"Damn!" I said, dropping into a chair. "I wish to God Mason had told Marshall what the hell it was he found. He didn't leave us with any trail to follow."

We fell silent. I was really upset that we had come to such an abrupt end of our investigation, partly because I felt we owed it to our late friends to try to find out who killed them, and partly because, although I'm embarrassed to admit it, I enjoyed our little brushes with adventure. I once played down the notion that Mother and I are thrill-seekers, but as time went on it was becoming more and more difficult to deny the facts. Peter at least gave the impression of being reluctant to get involved in these escapades, but he always went along nonetheless.

"Wait a minute," said Mother, breaking the long silence. "There is one thing Marshall did tell you that we could follow up, even though I'll admit it's quite the long shot."

"What?"

"Mason was interested in Thailand. Maybe that's the key."

"But who knows why he was interested in it?" Peter said, forever trying to be the voice of reason. "He could've just developed an interest in exotic places. God knows I never thought I'd see him get interested in Washington, but he did."

"No," I said, getting at least lukewarm to Mother's idea, "he asked Marshall about Thailand only after Marshall told him that that was where the doll came from." I turned to Mother. "But I don't see how that gives us anything to follow."

Mother shrugged. "We could go to the Thai consulate."

"There's a Thai consulate in Chicago?"

"There are for most countries," Peter said.

Mother added with another shrug, "Maybe they would know what would be important about one of their imported dolls."

"Maybe," I said half heartedly, "but that *really* seems like a long shot."

"It's an idea," said Mother.

"And it's the only one we have."

EIGHT

S unday managed to pass without any of our other friends getting butchered, which made for a change. It was possibly one of the most frustrating days of my life, since we didn't hear back from Nelson (not that we expected the CIA to be working on the Sabbath), and we didn't think the Thai consulate would be open until Monday. Peter and I spent most of the day lounging in front of the television watching a marathon of Thin Man movies, and Mother spent it cooking dinner and pampering the damn dog.

When I woke up Monday morning Peter was just getting out of bed. I lolled around in bed while he went into the bathroom and took a shower. After a while the water stopped, and a few seconds later Peter emerged with his hair still wet and a kelly-green towel wrapped around his waist. I hate to think that the death of our two friends had somehow caused a power surge in my libido, but as I lay there in bed watching him get a fresh pair of shorts and socks out of the dresser drawer, I was struck again with how sexy he is. Then again, in the last week I'd seen all too clearly how quickly one's stay on this planet can come to and end, and it probably just made me cherish what I had all the more.

I rolled out of bed and crossed to Peter, coming up to him

from behind and slipping my arms around him. My fingers interlaced across his stomach and my thumbs toyed with the wet, dark hair. I rested my chin on his shoulder and he rubbed his cheek against mine. Looking at our reflection in the octangular mirror mounted on the dresser, I thought we weren't a bad-looking couple. Peter smiled. Apparently he could feel my excitement against him.

I smiled back and almost laughed. For Christ's sake, I was turning into a human dowsing rod! All I had to do was get in the general vicinity of my husband and my member started wagging. Ah well, I guess there are worse fates.

Peter turned around to face me and we kissed much more passionately than we ordinarily would before breakfast. When our lips finally parted, he said quietly in my ear, "I'm going to be late for work."

I smiled as I loosened the towel from around his waist. "You bet you are."

After our impromptu liaison, Peter and I ate a quick breakfast. Then he the left for work and Mother set about her usual ritual of Monday housecleaning. She gets an almost sensual pleasure from vacuuming, a fact that I find frightening. And the damn dog was following her around as she cleaned, wagging its tail like a mad thing as if they were playing some sort of fascinating game. Mother tolerated this with a great deal of amusement until he really started getting in the way, then with one stern look she was able to make the dog slink quietly to a corner from which he continued to watch her with an unwavering sense of awe. This is another effect that Mother has on a lot of men.

Since Peter and Mother were busy, I was relegated the chore of visiting the Thai consulate to see if this one tenuous thread would give us a lead.

"It's not here," I said to Mother as she switched off the vacuum.

"What?"

"The Thai consulate."

She crossed to me and looked over my shoulder at the phone book opened on my lap. "I don't think it would be under Thai, darling. It'll probably be under consulate or consular."

"What a minute," I said, something on the page catching my eye. "Look at this." I pointed to a listing for the Thai Import/Export Company of Chicago. "They could probably tell us more about an imported doll than the consulate could, don't you think?"

Mother pursed her lips and thought for a moment. "You're probably right."

The Thai Import/Export Company of Chicago was located in one of those faceless steel-and-glass office buildings that sprang up like fungus in the sixties. This particular building was on Dearborn just south of the river.

The directory showed that the company was on the twenty-fifth floor, and a quick ride on a whisper-quiet elevator brought me to their door in a matter of seconds. I don't know what I was expecting to find when I went into the office, but it certainly wasn't the flat industrial space I walked into. At least a dozen gunmetal gray desks were pressed closely together in two rows. All of the desks were occupied by men, all of whom were dressed like accountants and were feverishly scribbling as if they would be beheaded if they didn't finish their sums by closing time. The claustrophobic working conditions damn near took my breath away—literally. I felt slightly lightheaded and found myself trying to remember if Thailand was one of those places where families lived a hundred to a room.

I was rescued from my near-swoon by a delicate female voice which said, "May I help you, sir?"

The voice had come from the receptionist, whose desk was the only one turned sideways so that it faced the door. She had a round face that was bookended by matching spit curls.

"I'd like to see . . ." I started to say, then realized that I wasn't really sure who it was I *did* want to see. "I'd like to see whoever is in charge."

"Mr. Sukin?" the young woman asked.

"Yes." I tried to sound sure of myself, which could hardly have been effective, given the way I'd started out.

"Do you have an appointment?"

"No, I'm sorry. I actually just need to talk to him for a minute."

"May I ask what this is about?" she asked with the exact same inflection she'd had for each question.

"Yes. It's about a doll."

There was a sudden cessation of the scribbling, and all of the pseudo-accountants looked up in unison. I suddenly felt like the only woman in a Japanese prison-camp movie. Of course, their reaction might have been due to the fact that my request was so stupid.

"A doll?" the receptionist repeated, sounding only faintly incredulous.

"Yes. I need to ask him about porcelain dolls from Thailand . . . unless there's someone else who could talk to me. . . ."

I heard the pseudo-accountant's pencils start scratching away at their various papers again. They were like a classroom full of children who didn't want to be called on.

"No," the receptionist said, "I think perhaps it is Mr. Sukin you should talk to. Let me see if he is available for you. Your name, please?"

"Alex Reynolds."

She picked up a phone on her desk and pressed a button, and after a brief pause babbled something into the receiver in her own language. The only words I recognized were my own name. After another pause, she said something else which I took to be the Thai equivalent of "goodbye" or "all right" or something, then replaced the receiver.

"Mr. Sukin will see you," she said, rolling her black eyes up at me. "Go through that door at the back of the room."

She pointed past the rows of desks to a door that was painted gold.

"Thank you," I said with a slight bow. Then I mentally kicked myself. Two minutes talking to someone from Thailand, and suddenly I was acting like a character in a bad road company of *The Mikado*.

I went down the center aisle of the desks to the door, gave a single knock, and then entered.

The private office was much nicer than the outer one. I suppose that was to be expected. There was a dark red carpet and a row of windows that looked out on an older building directly across the street. I half expected to find dragons on the walls, but instead there was just bland wood paneling.

Mr. Sukin sat behind a huge desk that made him look smaller than he really was. He rose as I entered the room, came out from behind the desk, and gave me his hand, which was very small and rough. He then offered me a seat and went back to his place behind the desk.

"It is nice to meet you, Mr. Reynolds. We seldom have, I suppose you would call it, drop-in guests." His voice was deep and soft.

"Thank you, Mr. Sukin," I replied, trying to sound a bit more professional.

"Call me Dave," he said with a sudden, toothy grin.

"Dave?" Right after I said it I hoped to God I hadn't sounded as astonished as I felt.

He nodded. "It is my American name. You Americans are so informal, you like to use 'Christian names,' I believe. Unfortunately, very early on I discovered that people were stumbling over my real name. I thought it would be easier for them if I just let them call me Dave."

"That's very . . . diplomatic of you," I said, not really knowing what else to say. But since he'd stopped talking and was sitting there with his hands folded and his eager eyes pointed at me, I figured I was supposed to say something.

"Now," he continued, "Miss Bunyarat said that there was a matter you would like to discuss with me."

I blinked. For a minute I thought he'd said "Miss Bunny

Rabbit," and it was a few seconds before I realized he was referring to the receptionist by last name. *God,* I thought, *I really need to get out more often.*

"Yes. I was wondering what you could tell me about dolls."

"Dolls? Yes. She said you wanted to know something about dolls. I was intrigued. That is why I told Miss Bunyarat to send you in."

He was going to have to stop saying her name, or I was going to get a case of the giggles.

"What did you want to know about them?"

I took a deep breath. "I was just wondering if you knew if there was anything special about some porcelain dolls that came from Thailand recently."

His eyebrows knit slightly. "I'm sure that the dolls are of very high quality. We are very proud of all of the products that we make in my country, especially those that are handcrafted."

"Well, yes, I know. . . . I mean, I figured that."

"We have in our country what is called an 'old-fashioned work ethic.' " He continued to grin, but I got the impression he was making a veiled slight on the American work ethic.

I chose to ignore this. "What I meant was, do you know of anything peculiar about dolls that might have been shipped to America recently?"

"Peculiar?" He repeated the word as if it was new to him. "Why do you ask?"

I sighed. I didn't know just how strange this was going to sound. "Well, a friend of mine—while visiting Washington— bought a porcelain doll that was made in Thailand. A few days ago he was killed, and that doll . . . along with his others, was smashed by whoever did it. We thought maybe there was something . . ."

His face become a mask of absolute amazement. "You don't think the sad death of your friend has something to do with a *doll?*"

I got the feeling that if I said yes he would be hard pressed to keep from laughing out loud.

"I don't know," I said haltingly, "I just thought maybe there was something important about that doll."

There was a pause, then he said, "We ship mil— thousands and thousands of products to this country. I wouldn't know anything about one single unit from one single shipment. And it doesn't even have to have been handled by my company. There are many, many importing companies from Thailand that operate in this country in many cities."

"Yes, but—"

"And you say there was something important about some doll, but you don't know what it was. I can't imagine what type of thing you mean."

"Whatever it was was worth killing over," I said somewhat tersely, but the light way he was taking this was starting to get on my nerves. Then again, what I was asking was so damn vague I don't know what other kind of response I could have expected. "I don't know," I said with a sigh, "I'm sorry. I'm not really sure what I'm looking for. It was the only lead we had, and I hoped you might know *something*. I guess I thought that if there'd been some sort of . . . I don't know, theft or crime or something over there—if something of value had been stolen and needed to be gotten out of the country, or into this country, you might know about it."

Here he bridled, and I can't say I blame him. It wasn't until I saw the hardened look on his face that I realized how what I'd just said must've sounded.

"You think that one of *my* people had something to do with the murder of your friend?" he said evenly.

"No," I said quickly, "I didn't mean—"

"Or that one of my people is involved in smuggling?"

"Oh, no, no!"

"This is a legitimate business, Mr. Reynolds." He sat back and folded his arms across his chest. "By what right do you come here with these obscene insinuations? Are you with the government, Mr. Reynolds?"

I'm not a very good liar (unlike some of my loved ones who

91

will remain nameless), so I said what I thought would sound the least elusive. "Do I *look* like I work for the government?"

"I don't know," he said, tilting his head as if he wanted to scrutinize me from a different angle. "Government agents, I understand, try not to look as if they are agents."

"Mr. Sukin . . . Dave . . . I assure you, I am not here on behalf of the government." I managed to make this sound very sincere, because it was, after all, the truth. "Look, I don't know if that doll really had something to do with my friend's murder. If it did, it doesn't have to have involved anyone from Thailand. Anybody could be responsible. All we know is that the doll came from Thailand."

For a moment he looked at me as if he thought I might be unbalanced, another thing that I couldn't exactly blame him for at that point. I must've sounded like some sort of nut. And I was beginning to feel like one, too. I had even less of an idea of what I'd hoped to find out here than when I started. But when you're grasping at straws, the straw looks pretty good until it starts to give way.

"We?" said Dave, raising his eyebrows. He'd gone from amusement to anger, but when he caught that one word he looked positively suspicious.

"My family and I," I said.

"Why would *you* need to find out about it?"

By now I had screwed the interview up pretty badly, but I thought just maybe I could allay his suspicions and get some information by falling back on grief.

"Well . . . you see . . . it's like . . . this was a very close friend of mine . . . the man who was murdered . . . and I'm trying to make some sense of his death."

Part of Mr. Sukin's smile returned: the part that curled up the right side of his mouth and made him look as if he were smirking at me.

"Ah, yes. Something that you find in Western religions."

"Huh?"

"In the East, we accept death, no matter how that death is achieved, as part of life."

"You're right," I said after a pause. "Here in the West we don't look at murder as an achievement."

He returned a tolerant, benign smile. "That is all right. I understand there are differences. I only wish that I could help you achieve peace. I'm afraid I cannot. I don't know anything in particular about any dolls, I only know that we are proud of all of our products in my country. I am very sorry about your friend, but you . . . if I may be so bold as to suggest it, I think you may have to learn to accept his death for what it is. I know that it can be a difficult lesson to learn, but it is a part of life. Perhaps it would help you to adopt the practice of meditation. Many people have found enlightenment by contemplating the idea of their own death."

He refolded his hands, the smile still in place. I was really perplexed. I had the odd feeling that he was threatening me. If that was the case, it was the most polite threat I'd ever gotten. He rose from his chair and put out his hand to me, making it clear that the interview was over. He then saw me to the door to his office. I could've sworn that the pencils were scratching harder at their work while Mr. Sukin stood in the doorway.

"I hope you may find peace," he said.

"Oh, I think I'll find what I'm looking for," I replied. I don't know why I made it sound like a challenge, except that I didn't like being put off, no matter how civilly it was done.

I walked away from him, feeling his eyes staring at my back along with the dozen pairs of eyes of the pseudo-accountants. It was like walking through a room full of those creepy paintings whose eyes seem to follow you around the room. The only one who didn't look up was Miss Bunny Rabbit, or whatever the hell her name was. She was doing her nails.

It was a relief to get out of there.

When I got home Duffy ran up to greet me at the door. He stared up at me with those big brown eyes, and with his little tail wagging so furiously it made me feel like a doggie bone.

"I'm sure Mother took you for a walk," I said. It was a split second before I realized I'd just referred to my mother as Mother to the dog. He came closer and butted his forehead against my shin.

"Oh, God," I said wearily as I reached down to pet him. His tail picked up speed.

"Darling, is that you?" Mother called from the kitchen. At the sound of her voice the dog sped to her side.

"Yes," I said, going in to join her.

"Did you find out anything?"

"Yeah. I found out how stupid I look trying to question someone without anything to go on. God, you should have seen the way the head of that place looked at me."

"Well, never mind," mother said with a wave of her hand. "Larry called while you were out. He said that Messrs. Dunn and Hamilton really are with the State Department."

"But of course he couldn't know whether or not the guys that came here really *were* Dunn and Hamilton," I countered.

Mother gave me a smile that was almost patronizing. "Don't be daft, dear. Anyway, he said they were with the State Department, and he doesn't know what they're working on but he made a point of telling me that we were to cooperate in any way possible with them." She stopped and a perplexed look came over her. "He made it sound as if he suspected that we wouldn't!"

I raised my eyebrows at her and she laughed.

"He *said* he didn't know what they were working on," I said, "but you know Nelson. He wouldn't tell us if he *did* know."

"Why keep it a secret?"

"Why keep anything a secret?" I said irritably. "These people are crazy. They live for secrets."

"He also said that we weren't to let them know that we've ever worked with the CIA," Mother added. "Now what do you make of that?"

I dropped into a chair at the kitchen table. "Nothing except that they're all more paranoid than I am."

"Where does that leave us?" said Mother.

"It leaves us nowhere." I sat for a moment in silence, then slapped my palm on top of the table. "Damn those people, anyway! I don't know what kind of game they're playing this time, but whatever it is it got Mason and Ryan killed, and I'm damned if I'm going to just let it go. Mother, we've got to find out what's going on."

"Rah-thur," she replied, emphasizing both syllables in an imitation of an upper-crust British character in a BBC miniseries. I'm never quite sure which of us she's making fun of when she does that.

The joint memorial service was held in the chapel part of the Merridew Chapel and Funeral Home, which was way up north on Clybourn. It was owned and operated by Randolph Merridew. It hardly seems possible to me that there could be such a thing as a gay mortician, since I'd bet that most of my brothers-and-sisters-under-the-sheets would shy away from any profession that would ensure they would never get laid. But Randy Merridew probably never had that problem. He was too good-looking. Far from the willowy, thin-voiced, creepy little morticians so popular in the movies and on television, Randy was a hulking, dark-haired brute who looked like he could cheerfully sling a body bag over his shoulder and whistle while he worked. Some guys find that alluring.

Randy had also earned the everlasting gratitude and respect of the gay community by readily providing the necessary duties for people who had died of AIDS at a time when many funeral homes were refusing them.

The building itself is really peculiar. It made of old, irregular gray stone, piled one on top of the other so that the building looks like an adjunct to a nonexistent castle. In the center of the front wall is a pair of modern glass doors that look completely out of place. A cave entrance would have been more fitting. I held the door open for Mother and Peter, then followed them in.

"Cor, there's a great turnout, in't there?" said Mother.

I shot her a dirty look to let her know I didn't think that was an appropriate observation, while blushing because I'd been thinking the same thing. The place was swarming with people, some of whom I knew and some I didn't.

"Makes you feel rather good to know that Mason and Ryan were so well loved. D'you know what I mean?" Mother added.

"Yeah," said Peter, slipping his hand into mine. "It's terrible that they're dead, but this makes you feel like no matter how they died, they didn't *live* in vain."

"Exactly. A show of love like this just shows that they enriched the world."

I found myself wondering if there would be more than two people at my funeral.

Randy noticed us almost right away, mainly because it's his job to do that, and he displayed a warm, compassionate smile as he headed for Mother.

"Mrs. Reynolds," he said, taking one of her hands in both of his massive palms, "it's so nice to see you again."

She smiled kindly at him and said, "Hardly seems proper, since you only see me at funerals."

"Ah, yes," he replied, the corners of his mouth turning down with practiced elegance, "this is a very, very sad occasion. And quite a shock. You never really expect anyone to die, do you?"

Before I could stop myself, I blurted out, "Well, *you* do, don't you?"

Peter's hand loosened and mother raised an eyebrow in my direction.

Randy smiled. "Ah, Alex, always the pragmatist. I meant you never expect people you know to die. But your point is well taken."

His eye suddenly caught movement by the front door and he was off to greet the latest arrival. Mother turned a disapproving eye at me and said, "I can't take you anyplace nice, can I?"

"I'm sorry. It just popped out."

The look in her eye told me that if anything else popped out of me, she might be tempted to pop it back in again. But after a few moments she relented and gave me a slight smile. "It's all right. Probably just the stress of this business."

Peter's hand retightened around mine.

We made our way through the throng in the foyer toward the doorway to the chapel. I spotted Marshall Torkelson up ahead. He saw me at the same time and nodded a greeting to me just as a young, earnest-looking woman with long brown hair hurried up to him. As we passed him, I heard the woman say, "Are you Mr. Merridew?" I had to clap my hand over my mouth to keep from laughing. With his cadaverous face, Marshall certainly looks more the part of an undertaker than Randy does.

Marshall gave a rather loud sniff and said through his nose, "No, I most certainly am not. He's over there." With which he pointed a bony index finger in the direction of the door, where Randy was continuing his hostly duties.

We had just about reached the doorway when a voice cried out, "Mother Reynolds, why it's you!"

Mother, Peter, and I stopped in our tracks and turned to find Stevie Sullivan approaching us from the side. Stevie is an old friend of Peter's. He's sort of like an old-fashioned tonic: easy to take in small doses and of questionable therapeutic value. But his heart is in the right place.

"Mother Reynolds, it's so wonderful to see you! It's been an *age!* An absolute *age!*" He threw his arms around Mother and squeezed her, which she accepted with as much grace as one can while having one's ribs crushed.

"Stevie, dear," she said when he released her, "you know I love you but if you don't stop referring to me as 'Mother Reynolds' I'll be forced to kill you. And I can do it, too."

Stevie grinned at her and his eyes goggled in that way that always reminds me of Tim Curry. "Why don't I just call you Sister Grenadine?" He wheeled around toward me and said, "Isn't it too, too terrible about Mason and Ryan? Just unbelievable!"

"Yes it is," I said in the sober tone I almost always adopt when talking to Stevie. I think it's compensation.

"And I understand that you're the one who found Ryan! How

awful for you! Especially since, from what I hear, he was sort of . . . inside out. My God, there's only so much you're supposed to know about your friends!"

"Yes, it was awful," I replied, "but how do you know so much about it?"

Stevie reared back and pursed his lips. "You must be joking! Tragedy goes through the gayvine like a brushfire!"

"Stevie," Peter said quietly, "would you please try to remember where you are?"

He looked startled for a moment, then abashed. "Oh, yes. Very serious. I forgot myself for a minute there. But don't you think . . . don't you think Mason would find this all a bit . . . well . . . funereal?"

I almost laughed. "As a matter of fact, I do."

"Well," Stevie continued, looking a bit relieved, "I just wanted to stop and say hi-de-ho to you and the Mrs. I have to move along. I'm trying to find my date."

Mother looked absolutely scandalized. "You brought a date to a wake?"

Stevie shook his head. "I didn't bring him, I met him here."

"What happened to the reformed skinhead you were dating? That's not still on?"

He rolled his bulging eyes so broadly they almost disappeared into the back of his head. "Oh, no, Alex dearest. He's off on his newest thing. He's found the Lord."

"You're joking."

"No, no, no," he said, shaking his head slowly and clucking his tongue. "Skinhead to skin flute to born-again Christian. When *will* that boy settle down?" He started to work his way away from us, but paused and said, "Oh, by the way, my new beau: He's a tiny little thing with tiny red hair. I can't find him for all these tall people! If you see him, send him my way. I'll be at the buffet."

"The buffet? There's a buffet?" Mother said, looking more scandalized by the minute.

"Oh yes, in the parlor. Assorted finger food. All the spring rolls you can eat!" With this he disappeared into the crowd.

Mother looked at me, her lips slightly drawn to one side. "An Asian buffet at a gay wake. What won't they do next?"

We went into the chapel and found seats near the back. The room was fairly large and subdued, with deep red, curtained walls that gave you a feeling of sobriety without religion. Up front there was a large wooden cabinet that resembled an altar, but not too much, and on it there was a display of flowers in the center of which were a pair of photos in gilded frames, one of Mason, the other of Ryan. They both looked exactly like they had when alive, happy and contented, an impish quality to their smiles.

As the rest of the mourners filed in and found seats, I became more and more uncomfortable under the gaze of the pictures. I started to get the feeling that they were looking at me.

"We know what you are," an amused voice said close to my ear.

"What?" I exclaimed softly, turning to my right.

Peter was looking at me. "I didn't say anything."

I looked back at Mason's picture and could have sworn his goofy smile was even wider.

"Why didn't you tell us, sweetie? What a lark! You're a secret agent!"

"Oh, Christ!" I said aloud.

"Honey, what's wrong?" Peter said.

Although I couldn't see Mother on my other side, I knew she was looking at me and I could feel her concern. I returned Peter's gaze and said, "I'm more stressed out than I thought I was."

"I know," he said, laying a comforting hand on my arm.

I leaned in toward him and whispered, "They know now."

"What?"

"Do you realize that? Mason and Ryan. They know now that we work for the government."

He looked back at me for a moment, then said quietly, "I suppose that's true. But they're not going to be telling anybody."

I turned back to the pictures. I wasn't too sure Peter was right.

"And since you're an agent, sweetie," Mason seemed to be saying, "you should be able to find out who did this."

Yeah, right, I thought.

The service was fairly short and sweet, with several of Mason and Ryan's friends giving them glowing testimonials and relating amusing anecdotes about their friendship. It kept the mood light, which I'm sure Mason in particular would have appreciated. I rolled my eyes at myself. I really hate it when anyone says they know what someone who has died would have wanted, and my two friends hadn't been dead a full week before I was doing it myself.

When the speakers had finished, someone produced a guitar and led the crowd in a rousing chorus of "Sleigh Ride," hopelessly incongruous under the circumstances, aside from it being months till Christmas, but it was Mason's favorite song. On more than one occasion he'd almost met an even earlier death at the hands of friends when they'd caught him whistling that peppy Christmas song in the dead of summer. Even though there were smiles on everyone's faces as they sang, it was the first time that people looked truly sorrowful.

When the singing had ended, the crowd disassembled into a milling mass, much in the way a congregation does after church.

"That was lovely, wasn't it?" said Mother. "They would have loved it, don't you think?"

"As much as you could love a funeral, I guess."

"They've formed a receiving line up there," she said, motioning to the "altar." The LaPeres and the Mortons had gathered and were shaking hands with the guests who were filing by, offering their condolences.

"We should go and greet the families," said Peter.

"Wait," I said. "You go on ahead."

"What is it?" Mother asked.

I pointed to the young woman who was just shaking hands with the last in the line of Morton family members. She was dressed in a tight-fitting black dress that didn't quite reach her knees, a broad black hat with a veil of a very open weave hanging down over her face, and she was propped up in a pair of killer heels. She was accompanied by another woman who was dressed in a similar fashion to a far less dramatic effect.

"Linda Brown," I said. "We need to talk to her."

"We do?" Mother managed to infuse these two words with enough incredulity to knock me off balance.

"She knows something. You said that yourself. She knows something about Mason's murder, at least, and we need to find out what that is."

"Oh, yes, I remember," she nodded, "but this is hardly the time or the place."

"We might not get another chance."

"Darling, I know how you feel, but I'm not sure I want you nosing around where two people have been slaughtered."

With that British lilt of hers, she made it sound as if she thought I was going to play at a building site.

"You don't think you could stop me, do you?"

Mother drew herself up to her full height, which is pretty impressive when she's angry, and crossed her arms over her chest. She didn't say anything, but she raised her eyebrows and had a look on her face that she very seldom uses on me. It's a look that says she doesn't care how far into my thirties I've gone, or whether or not I'm an adult with a husband of my own, I'll never be too big that she couldn't take a wooden spoon to my butt.

"I didn't mean that quite the way it sounded," I said apologetically. "But there can't be any harm in just talking to her. If she really does know anything, I can tell Frank."

"She can bloody well tell Frank herself."

"She's not going to do that. You saw how scared she was the other day. She practically fled the apartment when we told her when Mason was murdered."

"Perhaps she was just being wise."

"Mother," I said, trying to produce a displeased look, "you've never run from a problem in your life."

She tilted her head slightly and gave me a smile that made me blush. "I've never fallen for reverse psychology, either." She sighed and gave me a dismissive wave of her hand, much like I imagine the Queen Mum gives her vassals. "Oh, all right. Go. Question. Have fun. Peter and I will give the family your condolences."

Having just been given license to sleuth by my mother, and feeling about as ridiculous as she'd probably intended, I turned to cross the room to the end of the receiving line where I'd last seen Linda, only to find that she'd disappeared. I quickly scanned the room and saw that wide black hat of hers gliding over the heads of the crowd and out the door. I followed, marveling at the fact that Linda could move so evenly on those absurd high heels she was wearing. I guess it takes practice, but I still couldn't see how anyone could do it without falling forward or falling off. My only personal experience of high heels was back in the seventies when they became a brief fad for men. The result was a broken wrist I received when I was just about to cross the street and stopped abruptly when the light changed. I should say my feet stopped. The upper part of my body kept going and I hit the pavement.

Part of the crowd had dispersed into the outer lobby, and I had to work my way through them to catch up with Linda. She managed to reach the doorway to the parlor where the buffet was laid out before I got to her.

"Excuse me, Linda?" I said, gingerly catching hold of her elbow.

She instinctively pulled her arm away as if she expected some sort of attack and wheeled around.

"What?" she said, her eyes widening at the sight of me. "Oh, it's you."

"Linda, I have to talk to you."

She searched the crowd, apparently looking for help. "Ronnie? Where's Ronnie? I thought she was right behind me."

"It's all right," I said in a tone I hoped was calming, "I just want to talk to you."

"I don't . . . I don't know why you would. I don't know you, really." She fumbled in her black patent-leather purse and withdrew a lace handkerchief. She reached up under her veil and dabbed at her eyes.

"Look, it's obvious that you're scared. You should talk to somebody."

"I talk to Ronnie," she whimpered.

"I mean somebody official."

She blinked her big, wet, doe eyes at me, which was enough to show that she didn't know where *I* fit into that equation.

"Are you afraid to talk to the police? My mother and I know someone on the force, so we can help, if that's it. If you'll just tell me what it is, *I'll* go to the police for you. You won't have to go."

"Are you crazy?" she said, taking a backward step away from me and somehow still managing to stay balanced on those heels. Her face had lost that petite lustre and was staring at me as if she thought I might be dangerous. "If I *knew* anything, the police are the *last* people I'd want to know about it."

"But why? You don't have anything to hide, do you?"

"Of course not," she replied. She pressed the hanky to her nose and gave a genteel snort. "Except . . . I'm afraid for my life! If the police knew . . . everybody would find out about it and I'd . . . I'd . . ."

Her eyes brimmed over with tears and I realized just how terrified she really was. She raised the hanky to her nose again and gave a very indiscreet honk.

I was completely nonplussed. Linda gave every indication of wanting or needing to be comforted, but I don't exactly have a lot of hands-on experience with women. I put my arms around her, careful not to hold her too tightly, and gently patted her back. I probably looked like I was trying to burp her.

I happened to glance over at the buffet and saw Stevie looking at us. He was just picking up a piece of spring roll, and when he caught my eye he raised his eyebrows, formed a little *o* with his lips, then in one swift move popped the roll in his mouth and turned away.

"Well, how about this," I said quietly to Linda, who showed no sign of backing away from my tentative embrace, "why don't you tell me what you know, and I *won't* tell the police for you."

"Why should I do that?" she blubbered in my ear.

"Because maybe there's something I can do to help."

She let out a shivering sob, then straightened up and pressed the now sopping hanky against her cheeks several times, apparently trying to dab away the tears without smearing her makeup.

"Well . . . well . . . okay." She paused and looked to her left, then to the right to make sure nobody was listening. "The day Mason was killed . . . it was about four o'clock . . . I heard him cry out."

"You did?"

"Yes. It was like . . ." She widened her eyes, pursed her lips and let out an elongated "ooooh." "It was very short, but pretty distinct."

I could feel my forehead creasing. "You didn't go down to see what was wrong?"

"Of course not," she exclaimed with a mortified blush. She leaned closer to me and said, "Mason and Ryan were . . . sometimes . . . noisy." She turned her head away and her cheeks became even redder, but she managed to shoot me a glance out of the corner of her eye. She seemed to be waiting for me to get her drift.

When I finally realized what she meant, I said, "Oh . . . oh!" I cleared my throat. "But you didn't hear anything like china breaking?"

"No, but I wouldn't hear anything going on in the back of their apartment when I'm in the front of ours. Our apartment is just like theirs. Same layout. And I was in the living room. It wasn't until I went back to the kitchen that I heard him cry out."

She stopped and sniffed. When I realized she wasn't going to go on, I said, "Is that all?"

"What do you mean?" she said with a wide-eyed blink.

"I mean, is that all? I don't see how hearing a cry would put your life in danger."

She looked down at the floor like a guilty child, then back up at me. "Well . . . I saw something," she whispered very softly.

"What?" I said, matching her tone.

"Our kitchen window looks out over the back yard. Not long after I heard the cry, I saw two men going across the yard and out of the alley."

"And you didn't think anything of that?" I asked incredulously.

"Not at the time! They were dressed far too nicely for murder. Gray suits. They looked perfectly respectable." Her tears started to flow again. "And, you see, when you told me that Mason was murdered, at first I thought it had been at night, when Ronnie and I were away. But then you told me that it happened earlier, and I realized that must've been what I heard! I've been so . . . frightened." Her voice caught in her throat and the last word was released with a hiccup in between syllables.

"And you didn't tell the police?"

"No!" she exclaimed loudly, then she lowered her voice again. "I was trying to decide what to do, and before I did—decide, I mean—Ryan was killed. That's what's got me so scared!"

She started to weep openly, and before I knew it she was in my arms again. I managed to ask her one last question.

"Could you describe the two men?"

She shook her head with her face till pressed against me. I just knew that once I was out of this clutch my suit coat was going to look like a piece of modern art.

"No. I only saw them for a second and that was from behind. I never saw their faces. From the back they looked perfectly respectable."

Perfectly respectable . . . gray suits . . . I repeated to myself, a light dawning that I wished I could put out.

"This guy bothering you?" said a husky female voice to my left.

I turned my head and saw a woman considerably shorter than Linda (although that could have been mostly heels), clad in a similar black dress but without the hat. I recognized her as Linda's partner, Ronnie. Ronnie's complexion was ruddier than Linda's, and peppered with freckles, and if she was wearing any makeup at all it was only a touch of pale lipstick.

"Oh, Ronnie," Linda said as she transferred herself from my arms to her partner's.

"What've you been doing to her?" Ronnie demanded of me over Linda's shoulder.

"Nothing. I was just trying to help."

Ronnie snorted. "You did a great job." She stroked Linda's hair and tenderly cooed, "It's okay, baby."

"I'm sorry," I said helplessly, "I didn't mean to upset her. But . . . listen, are you two still staying in your apartment?"

"Hell no," said Ronnie, "We're staying out at my mother's till we can find another place. I don't think anybody'll hold us to our lease." There was a sardonic grin on her face when she said this. The callousness of it made my skin crawl.

"Good," I said, "because I don't think you're safe there."

"No shit," Ronnie said with another snort. "But anybody tries to cut up one of *us*, and he'll be sorry!" I noted the emphasis on the "he."

I can believe that, I thought as I went back to find my loved ones.

NINE

In the car on the way home I told Mother and Peter what Linda had said.

"Two respectable men in gray suits? I don't like the sound of that," said Mother.

"You'd rather they looked demented?" I said.

"I'd rather they *didn't* look like the two gents that visited us right after Ryan was killed," Mother said, wrinkling her nose at me in the rearview mirror.

"Could they really be the same guys?"

"I hope not," said Peter, sweeping his dark locks back out of his eyes with his right hand. "I don't have a lot of faith in the government, but I wouldn't want to believe they'd just go around killing people to get what they want."

"It depends on what they're looking for," I countered. It was one of those rare occasions when I found our roles reversing.

Mother shrugged. "After killing two people in cold blood, I hardly think that they would stick at killing us. I mean, if Mr. Hamilton and Mr. Dunn were the men that Linda saw leaving the yard, would they then sit calmly in our living room and ask us about it?"

"If they were clever enough," I said.

"Honey, they work for the government," Peter said with an ironic smile.

Mother sighed impatiently. "My point is, I would think they would've just killed us!"

We fell silent for a few moment. We'd finally reached our own neck of the woods and Mother made the turn onto Fullerton that would bring us back to our humble townhouse.

"An object," she said out of the blue.

"What?" I said.

She took a deep breath. "Well, doesn't that strike you as an odd way of putting it? They kept referring to what they thought Mason had obtained as 'an object.' Why wouldn't they tell us what it was?"

"Probably just more of that 'need-to-know-basis' crap that Nelson is always handing us," said Peter.

"Possibly," Mother replied, "but I think we need to look at this logically. It couldn't have been anything silly like microfilm because it had to be something that Mason could recognize on the spot."

"Not necessarily," I said. "He had that doll for several days. He had time to examine whatever it was he found."

"But you have to remember what he did when he found it, darling."

"What?" I said, getting irritated with myself that I didn't understand.

"He took it to Marshall Torkelson," Peter said to me. Then he turned to Mother and added, "But Marshall said Mason just showed him the doll, not anything else. Why not just have whatever it was appraised?"

"Exactly," said Mother, beaming at him as if she was confident it would come to him if he gave it time.

And it did. His face brightened suddenly and he said, "Oh, I see . . ."

"What?" I said.

"He asked Marshall about where the doll came from," Peter

explained, "because he was trying to find out the value without letting anybody *know* exactly what he had."

"Oh, great," I said, rolling my eyes. "Mason and Ryan wouldn't say what it was, Dunn and Hamilton wouldn't tell us what it was, the Thai import people don't know what it was, and the police don't know anything about anything. So how do we find out what the hell this thing is that's so important?"

"Intrinsic value," Mother mused, considering the words that Hamilton had used. "Something of intrinsic value. But it had to be something valuable enough that Mason could tell it was worth something. It's a riddle—rather like those logic problems they used to give at school. You know what I mean? Two trains leaving different stations at the same time, and when will they meet?"

"Yeah," said Peter, "only in those problems the trains weren't going to kill somebody if you didn't figure it out."

Mother steered the car into the alley and clucked her tongue as she is wont to do whenever we approach the rather ramshackle structure that serves as our garage. She must have some measure of affection for it as it stands, though, because she certainly has enough money to fix it if she wants to. Just as we pulled up behind the garage, I glanced at our townhouse and saw and faint flash of light.

"Wait a minute!" I said. "Quiet!"

"Quiet? What are you talking about?" Mother said. "We're not making any noise."

"Shhh! Did you see it?"

"What?" said Peter.

"There's somebody in the house."

Both of them turned in unison and looked out the windshield, which was useless because the garage was now blocking the view.

"How do you know?" Peter asked.

"I saw a light, just for a second."

"Are you sure?" said Mother, looking over her shoulder at me.

"Yes. It swung up for just a second and back down again. It must be a flashlight."

"Lor'," said Mother, wide-eyed.

The atmosphere in the car had suddenly become extremely tense, as if the knowledge of someone going through our house made us all feel that we weren't safe anywhere, even in the car. Without another word, Mother popped open her car door.

"What are you doing?" I demanded in a loud whisper.

She paused and looked back at me. "Well, we can't stay here."

I grabbed her shoulders. "Are you out of your mind? You can't go in there."

She looked at me as if I was clearly mad. "I can go next door to Mattie's and call the police."

"And tell them what? That our home is being invaded by someone looking for something that we're not supposed to have?"

"Darling, you make me dizzy when you talk like that."

"I'm serious."

"Well, what exactly do you think we should do? Just sit here in the bleedin' car and let them get away?"

I thought for a minute, then said, "No. I want to get a look at whoever it is that's in there."

"You really *are* mad," said Mother. Her eyes were still wide but all the humor had gone out of her expression.

"No, I'm not. Even if you call the police, whoever's in there will probably be gone by the time they get here, and I want to see who it is."

"I can bloody well guess who it is!"

"Who?"

Peter looked over the back of the front seat at me. "Dunn and Hamilton."

"The guys from the State Department? Why the hell would they be searching our house?"

"Why should be obvious," said Mother, curling the right side of her lips.

"I mean, why does it have to be them? It could be anybody!"

"They're the only ones who know we're involved in this."

"We're not involved in anything," I protested.

"The fact that someone is going through our home right now

would indicate that you're wrong."

I conceded the point by rolling my eyes digustedly.

"Alex, the only time our house has ever been burgled is when you've gotten us involved in these little episodes."

"That's not fair! I did *not* get us involved in this." My tone was more indignant than I had ever used with Mother before. "I'll admit that I was responsible for a couple of . . . unfortunate . . . things . . . but this is not my fault. If anything, it's Mason's fault for buying that damn doll!"

Mother raised her eyebrows. I had clearly stepped over the line. "Oh, I say, that's *very* un—"

Peter interrupted with a sigh. "Do you think that the two of you could possibly work this out when we're in a little less danger?"

Both of us looked at him. Mother laughed lightly. "Sorry, Alex. It's looks like you're not the only one being affected by all the stress."

"No, it was my fault. I shouldn't have—"

Peter cleared his throat. "Could you work that out later, too? There are people searching our house!"

The three of us looked back toward the house for a moment in silence. After giving it some thought, I said, "All right, Mother, go call the police. But while you're doing that I'm going to go up and try to get a look at who's in there."

"Like hell!" Mother exclaimed.

"I'm with Jean," said Peter, forever attempting to be the voice of reason when I sound like I'm about to do something really stupid. "We should just call the police, and hope they get here in time to catch whoever's in the house. If it's the guys from the State Department, then they can explain the whole thing to the police, and we can just claim ignorance."

I sat back in my seat. "You guys don't understand. It may not be Dunn and Hamilton. It might be the killers, trying to find the thing they were trying to get from Mason and Ryan."

"That's more of a reason not to go near there!" Mother exclaimed. Then suddenly her expression cleared. "But what am I thinking? It can't be them. They wouldn't know that we have anything to do with this, would they?"

Peter said, "You're not saying he should do this crazy thing!"

"Oh, no," Mother replied so offhandedly that neither of us was sure that she hadn't been suggesting it.

"Look," I said as I opened the car door, "you stay here and I'll just go up there and see if I can't get a peek at who's in there."

"No, Alex, I really wasn't—"

"I'll be fine. Don't worry. Peter will be with me."

"I will?" said Peter with one eyebrow raised.

I looked at him for a moment. "Well, you wouldn't want me going up there alone, would you?"

He frowned. Even a frown looks beautiful on that face. "You know, I've often secretly hoped that someday, if anything ever happened to one of us, we would die together, just because I didn't think I'd ever want to face life without you."

"Really?" I said, barely able to keep my voice from quavering.

"Yeah," he said, quietly opening the door on his side of the car, "but that was before I knew you were going to keep gleefully leading us into the valley of the shadow of death!"

We both climbed out of the car, and before softly closing the door I looked in at Mother and said, "You stay here."

"Of course," she replied with one of those enigmatic smiles that make me fear for the fate of mankind.

Peter and I slipped around the corner of the garage and made our way along the side. When we reached the front, I peeked around the corner as surreptitiously as I knew how, and Peter looked over my shoulder. There wasn't a repeat of the light. If there was still someone in there, and if it hadn't been my imagination, then whoever it was seemed to be making certain they didn't make any more mistakes.

I glanced at Peter and he nodded. Then we ran quietly across the back lawn, keeping low, and came to a stop by the back of the house, crouching on either side of the screen door to the porch.

I gave Peter a look that was supposed to ask "what do we do

now?" but in the darkness he couldn't see me. The kitchen windows were a bit too high for us to look in with any ease, and I don't think either of us wanted to take the risk of going around to the side windows for fear that the movement would be noticed. I still didn't see a repeat of the light. Our only real hope was the window in the back door which opened onto the porch, but that meant going up four stairs and through the screen door.

When we had remained crouched there for what seemed like an eternity, at least to my calves, I signaled Peter that I was going to move. I started up the stairs, still staying as low as possible. I closed my eyes and squinched my face up as I turned the handle on the screen door, as if that would make the door open more quietly. I managed to pull it open with only a faint squeak, and moved onto the porch.

I was still holding the door open as Peter reached out for it to follow me in. I let go of the door thinking that he had it, but I was wrong. In one of those sickening moments of realization you get when you know that you've just made a really big mistake, I felt the door swinging shut. It closed with a loud bang before I could turn to catch it. Through the screen, Peter's face looked as startled as I felt. I whispered "Oh, shit!" and plastered myself against the door under the window. Likewise, Peter pressed himself against the wall outside the screen door and looked like he'd like to disappear into it.

I had my ear to the door and couldn't hear anything at first. But then there seemed to be a quiet rush within the house away from the back door. I guessed that whoever was in there was making a hasty departure through the front door.

I eased myself up and took a deep breath before peeking through the window. Ever since seeing that *Twilight Zone* episode with William Shatner on the airplane I've harbored this secret fear that if I peek through a window there'll be a gremlin staring back at me from the other side. It's irrational, but I saw that show when I was little, and these things stick with you. Anyway, with the deep breath in my lungs I forced myself up to look through the window and saw nothing: no gremlin and nobody else, either.

But I thought I heard the front door open.

"I think they're gone," I said to Peter, who pulled away from the wall and came up onto the porch.

I fitted my key in the lock and turned it, but found that the lock had already been opened. I don't know why that made my heart sink, since we already knew that somebody had been in there. We rushed into the kitchen and through the house to the front door, which our burglars had left ajar in their rush to get out.

We ran down the front steps and to the walk, and then looked both ways down the street.

"They went that way!" Mother's voice came from the shrubbery beside the narrow walk between our house and our neighbor's.

"What?"

She came out to join us. "They went that way," she repeated, pointing east.

"What the hell are you doing here? I told you to stay in the car!"

She placed her hands on her hips and frowned. "Are you going to stand there nattering at me, or are you going to follow them?"

Peter and I ran off in the direction that Mother had indicated, figuring that in order to have disappeared so quickly they must have turned off at the first side street. But when we got to the end of the block and looked, nobody was there. Not that we expected there to be. Our exchange with Mother hadn't been long, but it had been enough for whoever had been in our house to disappear.

As we walked back to the house I felt a chill run up my spine. Our house had been invaded before, but we'd never been there when it happened. It was really unsettling to not only know that your house has been broken into, but to almost stumble into the people who did it.

When we entered the living room I was surprised to find that the house was none the worse for wear. Whoever was searching it was being careful about it, which oddly enough made me feel a bit relieved. Knowing how destructive the killers had been at Mason and Ryan's apartment, I guess this gave me hope that they weren't the ones who'd broken in here. We found Mother dialing the phone.

"Are you calling the police?" Peter asked.

"No, I'm calling that bloody Larry Nelson."

"Nelson? Why?" I said.

"Oh, by the way," she said as if she hadn't heard the question, "I checked. The bag of doll-leavings is still there. They didn't find them. But I couldn't find Duffy."

"Why are you calling Nelson?"

"Because I'm damned if I'll have those damned government people breaking into our house!" she exclaimed, holding the half-dialed phone out at me as if it was somehow involved in the break-in. "And I intend to tell Larry Nelson just that!"

"But he doesn't have anything to do with the State Department."

"Not 'alf," she said, not particularly making sense but dropping her aitches as she is wont to do when she's truly upset. "But they're all connected somehow. He bloody well better be able to do something about this."

"Mother, we don't know that it was Hamilton and Dunn."

"Who else could it be? Nobody else knows that we had anything to do with Mason and Ryan."

"But you didn't see them, did you, Jean?" Peter asked.

"No. I didn't get there in time. I held back until I heard the door slam, then lit quick as I could up to the front walk. I thought perhaps they'd go that way."

"Mother, you might've run into them!"

"Well, what of it! I belong here, they don't!"

"But they might've—"

"Did you see anything?" Peter chimed in, cutting me off.

"I was only halfway there when they ran past. I just saw a flash of them. I didn't get to see who it was but I know there was more than one of them."

She looked back down at the phone and realized that she'd

forgotten how far she'd gone in dialing Nelson's number when we interrupted her. She pressed the disconnect button, then started dialing again.

"Mother, it's after eleven in Washington. Nelson's not going to be there."

"It's a cellular phone," she said none-too-softly, "he doesn't have to be *there*, he just has to be in his pants. Let's hope he is."

"I'm sure he is," said Peter. "I can't imagine that he has any social life. I'll see if I can find the dog."

Peter has never been overly fond of Agent Lawrence Nelson. I didn't know whether that was out of a personal dislike or whether it was from the general distrust he felt toward anyone in the government. Hell, we'd known Frank O'Neil for years and Peter still didn't quite trust him, mainly because he was on the police force.

"Larry?" said Mother sharply. Apparently Nelson was still with his pants. "Listen, what's up with you, eh? What d'you mean having government agents break into our house and search it?"

She listened for a moment, and the look on her face was definitely not amused. Then she said, "Now you listen to me, Larry Nelson, you told us that those two men—that Hamilton and Dunn—really do work for the State Department. If that's true then it's *your* people who just broke in here . . . All right, they're not your people, but they're government people. They're the only ones who know about— Yes, I know that, but it had to be them. Who else could it be?" She listened again, then curled her lips and said witheringly, "Ha ha." She put her hand over the mouthpiece and looked at me. "He said that, knowing us, it could be anyone."

"Ha ha," I replied, imitating her.

"I want something done about it," she said into the phone. "Straightaway, do you understand?"

She now went silent for an extended pause. Her expression relaxed somewhat, but instead of looking relieved she looked worried. She then straightened herself up and said, "Of course we don't know."

"What is he asking you?" I said.

She put her hand over the mouthpiece again and whispered, "He wants to know if we know what they were looking for." When I raised my eyebrows, she added, "I'm not lying, we really don't."

She took her hand away and said into the phone, "Well, I would very much appreciate it if you would!" Then she hung up.

"You'd appreciate if it he'd what?" I asked.

"He said he'll try to find out just what it's all about and let us know," she said. Then she heaved a heavy sigh. "Maybe he can find out something from his end. Lord knows we've been stymied on ours."

"Except we know that we've done something, or they wouldn't have come here."

Mother rolled her eyes. "Darling, we haven't *done* anything. We don't *have* anything, and we don't *know* anything. That doesn't mean they don't *think* we do. You know that as well as I do!"

At that moment Peter came down the stairs, holding the previously missing dog in his arms.

"Where was he?" Mother said with a broad smile. She took both of his cheeks—the dog's, not Peter's—in her hands and gave him a loving shake.

"He was hiding under your bed."

"It figures," I said.

"Oh, the poor doggie," said Mother.

"Great watchdog."

"He's not supposed to be a watchdog," Mother said, pressing her forehead against the dog's. "*We're* supposed to look out for *him.*" She gave his head a scratch, straightened up, and said, "All right, that's enough of that. I know you've been scared, so let's take you out and give you a biscuit, eh?"

With that, Mother headed for the kitchen with the dog scrambling at her heels. I looked at Peter and said, "There was a time when our lives were in danger that she'd look after *me.*"

Peter grinned. "Do you want a biscuit, honey?"

I slapped his shoulder. "I'm going to go put the car away."

I went out through the back door, across the yard, and down

the walk alongside the garage to the alley. In Mother's haste to catch a glimpse of the criminals, she'd left the driver's-side door open and the motor running. I spared a thought for how lucky we were that the car hadn't been stolen on top of everything else that had happened.

I was just climbing into the driver's seat when a soft voice spoke out of nowhere.

"Mr. Reynolds?"

I jumped from the car as if it were haunted and peered in the window to the back seat. There was nobody there.

"Mr. Reynolds?" The voice came again, from the general vicinity of the garage. A slender Asian man stepped from the shadows by the garage door.

"Jesus Christ! Where did you come from?"

"I'm sorry if I startled you," he said quietly, stopping just short of coming into the light thrown by the overhead lamp on the other side of the alley. "I wanted to talk to you."

"Who are you?"

"That doesn't matter."

I peered through the relative darkness at him. "You look familiar. You were at that Thai import company, weren't you?"

He nodded. "Yes. I was there when you paid your visit."

"Why are you here?"

"I came because it is important that I talk to you."

I turned my head doubtfully, keeping my eyes on him. "Most of our visitors come to the front door."

There was a hint of a smile on his face. "It was apparent . . . when I arrived . . . that your house was occupied by someone other than its proper tenants. I thought it best to wait somewhere out of the way."

"Did you see who was in the house?"

"No," he replied with a slight shake of his head, "I'm afraid not. I was back here, and their retreat was rather hasty, wasn't it?" He seemed to find that amusing.

"What did you want to talk to me about?"

He looked down at the ground, then up at me. "I want to

talk to you about what you found."

"What are you talking about? I didn't find anything."

I thought I detected more than a hint of a smile this time. "Though I wouldn't want you to think I meant any disrespect to my superior by what I am about to say, I'm afraid that Mr. Sukin lied to you when you visited him this morning."

"Lied about what?"

There was a pause, then he said, "About the doll, Mr. Reynolds. About the doll that you came to ask him about."

"How do you know he lied?"

"Because when a . . . certain item was stolen in my country, all of the importers of Thai goods—particularly dolls—were notified to be on the lookout for it. That is how I know that Mr. Sukin knew what you were referring to."

Actually, when I asked the question I had wanted to know how the guy knew what Sukin had said to me at all. But I thought it would be better to let that pass.

"I'm afraid I still don't know what you're talking about."

He sighed. "You must know something, or you wouldn't have known to come to us."

"All I knew for sure was that the doll came from Thailand. I don't have any idea why the doll was so important." From what I could see of his face, I was certain that he didn't believe me. "Perhaps you could fill me in." I added this because I thought it might convince him that I really didn't know, and also might get him to give me some information.

He looked back down at the ground for such a long moment of silence that for all I knew he could've been giving a silent prayer for guidance. Then he looked up and said, "A certain item is believed to have come into the possession of your friend. Your friend who was killed." He said this last bit slowly, to give it more emphasis.

"I thought that much," I said impatiently, "but what is it?"

He hesitated, then said, "It is an item of sufficient significance to make it almost invaluable."

Again he wanted to dance. I wondered if any of these people

would ever realize that if they would just come out and tell you what the hell they were talking about, you might be able to help them.

"So it's worth a lot of money," I said, trying to draw him out. I didn't want to make him angry, because I figured I could get more information out of him if I could keep him talking.

"It is of a certain financial value," he replied somewhat stiffly, "making it a worthwhile object, I suppose, to vend on the open market . . . if one is able." There was something in his tone that made it clear he didn't think anybody would live long enough to sell the thing. "But it has a value beyond mere monetary considerations that makes it, I should say priceless."

"Now, what could that be?" I said with enough sarcasm to let him know that I was tired of going around in circles.

He bowed his head briefly, then said, "It is an artifact of *religious* significance."

He stopped, apparently to let this sink in. Which it did. It brought back Billings's questions about whether Mason and Ryan were involved in some sort of religious cult or something. Being eviscerated. The police seemed to think that meant it was some sort of religious doings. And it looked like they were right.

"But what *is* it? How am I supposed to know whether or not I've seen it if I don't know what the hell it is?"

The smile reappeared. "You would know it if you saw it. As I'm sure you know."

"I don't know anything," I said testily, "and I haven't seen any religious icon."

"It was believed that the item was in the possession of your friend. . . ." he said slowly, ". . . It is now believed it has come into your possession."

"My possession? Why?"

"Because you're known to have been asking questions about it."

"I asked questions about a doll," I protested, "not about some artifact."

There was a gentle, condescending laugh. "You asked ques-

120

tions about a particular doll."

"But still—"

"I beg of you, Mr. Reynolds," he said, not sounding a bit like he was begging, "if you have found the artifact, please, please turn it over to the authorities."

"The authorities? If somebody's willing to kill over it, wouldn't it be safer for me to turn it over to the people who are after it?" Immediately after I said this, I realized how it sounded. I quickly added, "I mean, if I had it."

"It doesn't matter. If you give it to the authorities it will be returned to its rightful place—the temple from which it was stolen. If it must be . . . recovered by its adherents, then things may not go so well for you."

Now he really was starting to scare me. "But why? Why would they want to hurt someone who wanted to give it back to them? I knew Mason really well. If he knew that whatever the hell this thing is was that important to somebody, then he would've given it back to them. Why would they kill him anyway?"

The man seemed to bristle in the relative darkness. I got the feeling I was digging my grave deeper and deeper. What I'd meant as simple questions he seemed to keep taking as proof that I had the blasted thing. His kept his voice even as he replied, "Because it has been *defiled*. It was holy, and it has been *defiled*. Please trust me when I say to you, Mr. Reynolds, that whoever has the item now is in the gravest of danger. Your life is worth nothing if you do not turn it over to the proper authorities immediately."

It didn't escape me that he'd gone from the abstract to the specific when he said, "your life is worth nothing." He really did think I had the thing.

"And I assure you that these people are ruthless, and will stop at nothing to retrieve what has been stolen from them."

"Who *are* these people?" I asked with frustration.

There was a pause, then he said in a whisper, as if he were afraid to be heard, "The Metanayans."

"What?"

At that moment, Peter called out from the back porch, "Alex?

What's taking you so long?"

I stepped to the side of the garage and called back, "I'm back here." When I turned back the Asian man had disappeared.

I was standing there gaping like an idiot at the space by the shadows where the man had been standing when suddenly a voice said, "What are you doing?"

"Jesus!" I cried out as I wheeled around, putting my hand on my heart. Peter was looking back at me with a big question mark on his face. "Don't do that!"

"Do what? What are you doing out here?"

I let my hand drop and sighed with relief. It wasn't until then that I realized I'd been trembling. "Apparently I'm doing *Mr. Moto* on location."

"What are you talking about?"

I told Peter all about the strange visitor, and he looked less than pleased.

"I don't like this," he said. "People breaking into the house and then this guy popping up back here. This is not good."

"That's an understatement," I said, dropping into the driver's seat of the car. I drove into the garage and Peter pulled the door down, closing himself inside with me.

I climbed out of the car in the darkness and joined Peter behind it, sitting myself on the trunk. "God, what a mess. It looks like whoever killed Mason and Ryan thinks that we've got whatever it is they're looking for."

"So, didn't this guy tell you what the hell it is that everybody's after?"

I shook my head. "No. Just that it's some sort of religious icon, so it could be anything from a statue of Mary to a side of beef. Who the hell knows? Christ, they keep calling it an 'item' or an 'object,' and we're supposed to divine from that what the damn thing is. It's like being in some psychotic game of *Password*."

"Except—"

I cut him off. "If you're going to say that in a real game of *Password* you don't get killed if you don't guess the right word, I don't need to hear it right now."

"Sorry," he said sheepishly. There was a pause, then he said, "Are you cold?"

"No," I said, realizing now that he'd pointed it out that I was still trembling.

Peter smiled and said, "Here," and put his arms around me and rubbed my back. I slipped my arms around his neck and pulled him closer, my lips meeting his.

We were silent for a few moments, content to enjoy the warmth of each other's closeness.

"Did you mean what you said?" I asked.

"About what?"

"About dying together."

He smiled. "Well, I don't want to do it anytime soon, but yes, I did. Morbid as it may sound."

I shook my head, still looking away from him. "It doesn't sound morbid to me."

He took my face in his hands, gently turning me to face him. "Have I told you lately how much I love you, and that you're the most important thing in my life?"

"Uh huh."

He laughed lightly. "Well, it's still true."

We kissed again, and went on kissing until there was a knock at the side door of the garage.

"Boys? Are you in there?"

We loosened our liplock and laughed, pressing our foreheads together.

"You know," I said, "when she does that I feel like I'm four-teen again."

Peter screwed up his face comically. "Were you bringing boys home when you were fourteen?"

I mussed his hair and called out, "Coming, Mother!"

"You mustn't disappear like that when we've been burgled," Mother said as the three of us walked back to the house. "First you coming out here and being gone for so long, then I send Peter out to find you and he doesn't come back. It's like to give one pause, you know."

"Sorry," I said. Then I told her about the surreptitious meeting with the Asian gentleman.

"Oh, dear," she said as we entered the kitchen. "Then it doesn't have to have been the boys from the State Department who broke in here."

"Not necessarily," said Peter. "But it still might've been them."

"Lord, I hope it was!"

Not twenty minutes earlier she'd been furious at the thought that it had been Hamilton and Dunn. Now she'd changed her tune. And I could easily understand why.

"I suppose I shall have to apologize to Larry," Mother said, broadening her accent.

"Don't you dare!" Peter and I exclaimed in unison.

TEN

When we came down to the kitchen the next morning, Mother was busily preparing breakfast. She was clad in an emerald-green kimono that was as plain as something that shimmers can be. That is to say, it's the only one of her many kimonos that is practically devoid of embroidery, except for around the hem and the cuffs: no dragons, no pagodas, just that glimmering green fabric. It always amazes me that she can flip things around the stove with several burners going and never set fire to those voluminous sleeves.

We had scrambled eggs, sausages, and toast, a combination that is just as likely to send me back to bed as prepare me for the day. And we were just clearing the table when the doorbell rang.

"I'll get it," I said, leaving Peter to finish his coffee and Mother loading the dishwasher.

I took a quick peek through the curtains—a habit learned from Mother—to see who was there before opening the door. To my surprise Mr. Dunn and Mr. Hamilton, the agents from the State Department, were standing on the front stoop staring dully at the door. They looked as if they weren't quite sure whether they wanted it to open or not.

I rounded the corner and opened the door.

"Well, look who's here. It's the feds!" I yelled this over my shoulder.

"Can we speak with you and your family?" said Mr. Hamilton, who seemed to be in the habit of speaking before his partner.

"About what?"

"About what happened here last night."

"What? Didn't you find what you were looking for?"

Hamilton looked down at the ground and sighed heavily, then looked back up at me. "Mr. Reynolds, may we come in?"

"If I didn't want you to, that wouldn't stop you, would it?" I said, stepping aside and waving them past me.

"That's what we want to talk to you about," said Dunn.

"Then you'd bloody well better start talking," Mother said sharply. She was standing in the kitchen doorway, her hands balled into fists and firmly planted on her hips, and a scowl on her face that I would've known meant trouble even if I hadn't known her. Peter came up behind her and watched over her shoulder.

"Mrs. Reynolds, we did not break into your house," said Hamilton. "That's what we came to tell you."

"Oh, really?" Mother said with a triumphant smile as she advanced into the room. "And how exactly did you know we thought you'd done it?"

"We've been informed that it was suspected that we'd been involved in some illegal activity connected with your house."

"Oh, God!" I said rolling my eyes. "I know we're in trouble when you guys start talking like that."

"We really are on the same side, Mrs. Reynolds," said Hamilton, pointedly ignoring me.

"I'll reserve judgment on that until I know for sure whether this is your second or third visit to this house."

He sighed again. Apparently it was the only way he had of conveying irritation. "We have also been informed that it might be time for some interdepartmental cooperation."

So that was it. Nelson had gotten on to them, or someone

else had on his behalf, and now they thought that they could trust us. I wish I could've felt the same way about them, but by then we'd had far too much experience to ever take anyone at face value.

"Interdepartmental cooperation?" said Mother, her voice getting higher and taking on a slightly mocking edge.

"Yes."

"Good," I chimed in. "Then maybe you can start by telling us who the Metanayans are."

For the first time Hamilton betrayed surprise. I mentally shook my head. It would've taken Agent Lawrence Nelson much longer to disclose any emotion. I figured Hamilton must have been fairly new to his job. He and Dunn glanced at each other, and neither of them looked pleased. Clearly Hamilton believed that interdepartmental cooperation meant that we would be cooperating with him, not the other way around.

"So," said Hamilton, "you've gone farther into this thing than you were willing to admit."

"We haven't gone anywhere," I replied, "we've stayed right here. This thing keeps coming to us."

"Now perhaps you could answer the question," said Mother.

"The Metanayans," said Hamilton, looking exactly as if he were sure we knew all of this already, "are a religious sect, mostly living in Thailand, although there are some smaller branches of it in other Asian countries."

"And in the United States?" said Peter.

"Yes."

Hamilton stopped and gave no indication that he was about to give us any further information. It was like talking to a desk reference.

"So?" I said.

"They are a violent offshoot of Buddhism," Hamilton continued, "worshipping in some of the same ways—"

"Wait a minute, wait a minute," Peter cut in, "Buddhists aren't violent."

Hamilton turned to him and said evenly, "That's why they're

an offshoot. Just like Lutheranism is an offshoot of Catholicism."

"I *hardly* think that's a good example," said Mother in her most withering British accent.

"Almost every religion develops a violent faction. There's always someone in the ranks who believes that violence is a way to achieve certain ends. The Metanayans are not naturally violent. They believe in peace and tranquility and all that stuff just like the Buddhists. They are only violent if provoked."

"Like the Jedi," I intoned.

"Alex, please," said Mother.

Hamilton looked at me and wrinkled his nose. "Protestants and Catholics aren't supposed to believe in killing people, either, but tell that to the Irish."

Mother visibly stiffened. The Irish are a touchy subject with her, although I have no idea why. I've always meant to ask her which side of the problem she comes down on, but I've never gotten around to it. Knowing her, her views are probably as pragmatic about that as they are about everything else.

"All right, all right," I said, trying to get back to the point. "So they are what they are. Why are they here and what are they after?"

Hamilton heaved his heaviest sigh yet. Apparently we were taking up much more of his time than he wanted to give us. Dunn was looking at Hamilton's face, waiting to take his cue.

"Could we sit down?" Hamilton said at last.

Mother waved them to the couch, and she and I sat across from them. Peter pulled up a seat beside me.

Hamilton crossed his legs and wrapped his hands around his knee. "It all has to do with the theft of a valuable object from the Metanayan Temple in Bangkok."

"An *object* again!" I said with no patience at all.

"The theft was done by a Mr. Robert Williams. He worked for a company called . . ." Hamilton looked to Dunn.

"Fotheringby Import/Export," Dunn said.

Hamilton turned back to us. ". . . a company based in Washington, D.C. They import things from all over the world. Mr.

Williams was one of their buyers."

"You keep speaking of him in the past tense," Peter said leerily.

"That's because he *is* in the past now. Mr. Williams stole the thing, but only got just so far away with it. He was found two days after the theft. He'd been killed in a ritualistic manner and dumped into the Gulf of Siam. Unfortunately, the object wasn't recovered there."

"You keep referring to this thing as an object," said Mother. "Don't you think it's about time you told us what it is?"

"You mean you don't know?" said Hamilton, once again showing genuine surprise.

"We know it's of religious significance," I said. "We don't know what it actually is."

Hamilton looked at Dunn, both of their expressions full of disbelief. It would seem that they had both been laboring under the impression that we actually had the thing and were holding out on them until they had placated us with what little goodies we wanted: in this case, information. But for the first time they looked as if they doubted why they were there.

Hamilton leaned back as Dunn leaned forward in that same bizarre scissor action they seemed to have worked out between them. Apparently it was Dunn's turn to talk.

"It is a diamond. A very valuable diamond. I'm told that it's flawless and has a natural violet cast to it. So it's very valuable in its own right, but even more so for its significance to the owners."

"You're *told* that," said Peter. "You've never seen it?"

Dunn smirked. "I've never been to Thailand."

Hamilton seemed to find that amusing.

They scissored again, and Hamilton took up the story. "Anyway, it appears that Mr. Williams heard about it, and took it upon himself to unofficially export it. He pried it from the navel of the Metanayan Buddha, and fled the temple with it."

"The Metanayan Buddha," I repeated slowly, emphasizing it in hopes Hamilton would see how ridiculous it sounded. I half suspected that once he had realized that we didn't have the diamond, he had begun putting us on. "A gem. Stolen from the navel of the Metanayan Buddha. Really. How very Bulldog Drummond."

Hamilton turned his narrowed eyes on me. "Is it? Maybe I should remind you that two of your friends have been murdered over it."

I was suitably abashed. It might sound like something out of a B picture, but I'd seen Ryan's body. It wasn't pretty.

"Exactly," said Mother. "How on earth did it go from being stolen in Bangkok to ending up in Mason's hands?"

Hamilton pursed his lips. He looked like he didn't see the need to explain any more to us, but after a slight pause he shrugged and went on. "Williams made a big mistake. Apparently he didn't know it was always guarded. From what we've been able to piece together since then, he was pursued from the temple, and managed to elude the people chasing him for only a brief period. After he was caught and they found that he didn't have the thing on him, he was executed. I don't know how they were able to find it out—and I don't want to know—but the place he had hidden when they lost him was a small warehouse where they make dolls for export."

"Oh . . ." I said, sitting up in my chair. The light was beginning to dawn. "I get it. He hid the diamond in one of the dolls and . . . what? Planned to just buy the dolls for his company and get it back when it had gotten to the states?"

"That's as good an explanation as any," said Hamilton. He almost looked impressed. "But the problem for the Metanayans was that by the time they discovered where the diamond had been hidden, the dolls were already on their way here. We weren't notified of it until after it had arrived."

"Who notified you?" Mother asked.

"The Thai government."

"Their government is involved?" Mother's forehead creased deeply.

"Their government is only interested in getting the thing back."

"Are you telling us that the Thai government is involved in the killings of three people?"

"Well," said Hamilton, his face showing that he thought any government outside of the United States would be capable of such a thing, "no, not really. The Thai government contacted us on behalf of the Metanayans. You have to understand that the Metanayans are a small cult, but they are very influential in the government. The government is only interested in getting the thing back. I wish I could say that of the Metanayans themselves."

"What do you mean?" said Mother.

"I mean that getting it back may not be enough for them. They may want more than that."

"Like revenge?" said Mother. "I'd think they'd bloody well had done with that!"

"They are zealots, Mrs. Reynolds. There's no accounting."

Peter's attention seemed to be grabbed by this. "Oh . . . oh, I don't like where I think this is heading."

"Huh?" said Dunn, animating again.

"I have a feeling that you're only interested in getting this thing back, too," he replied, his right eyebrow arching sharply.

"Of course we are," said Hamilton. "What else?"

"Mason and Ryan," I said indignantly. My face was hot, so I knew I'd turned red.

"What about them?"

He sounded so casual that I swear to God if I'd had a gun I would've shot him.

"They were *murdered* by these people," I said, leaning across the coffee table at the agents. "Do you think we'd be satisfied with just having you hand back to them what they're looking for and letting them go their merry way?"

There was a marked hesitation before he said, "I assure you that everything possible will be done to bring the perpetrators to justice."

I sighed and looked at Mother. "You know, everybody is assuring us of everything lately, and the more they do it the less sure I am!"

"It still doesn't make sense to me," said Mother, employing the knack for understatement that is part of her heritage. "Supposing the dolls *were* shipped to America? How on earth did the Metanayans know that it was in Mason's doll?"

"Apparently they didn't, at first. There were a hundred dolls. They were shipped to an import company in Washington—not the one Mr. Williams was employed by. Only five of the dolls had already left the company when the Metanayans arrived in pursuit. The import company was broken into, and all the dolls destroyed. That left five. Three of the five were still at the shop to which they'd been sold."

"A doll shop in Georgetown," I said.

"Yes," Hamilton replied after a beat.

"And the doll shop was broken into?"

He nodded. "The remaining dolls were destroyed, and we can only surmise that the owner of the shop told the Metanayans to whom the last two dolls were sold."

"You can only surmise?" Mother said. Her complexion had gone a bit pale.

"From the condition he was found in, I'm sure he told them whatever they wanted to know."

Mother swallowed hard. I couldn't swallow at all.

"And the other doll?" Peter asked.

"It was stolen from Mrs. Mary Conifer, and elderly woman living in Georgetown. She reported it stolen before we were even onto it. From what she said it was still in the gift-wrapped box from the store. She'd intended it as a gift to her niece."

"Hmph!" said Mother. "Good job she didn't open it. Or send it."

"That's right," said Dunn, nodding his head gravely. "It looks like the people after the diamond figured that if the diamond had been in that doll, Mrs. Conifer didn't know about it. And apparently it wasn't, because then they came after your friend."

"But if they didn't find the diamond in Mason's doll, why did they have to kill him?"

Hamilton shrugged. "Maybe just out of revenge. But I'd bet

that the diamond wasn't in the doll anymore. I'd bet your friend found it and hid it somewhere else."

I'm ashamed to say that Mother and I betrayed ourselves on this point. We exchanged glances, remembering that that was exactly the explanation I'd thought of earlier. It certainly wasn't comforting to have that particular theory verified.

"Which means," Hamilton continued broadly, "that the Metanayans are still on the trail of the diamond. And whoever has it is in a lot of danger."

He stopped, and both he and his partner looked at the three of us significantly, as if this was the time we were supposed to fess up and deliver the diamond.

"But we don't have it," said Mother, "and we never did."

"Are you sure?" Hamilton asked.

"Well, we bloody well would've noticed a violet-colored diamond big enough to fit in Buddha's navel!"

I almost laughed. That statement probably would've sounded just as ridiculous without the accent, but I doubt it.

"So you're not going to help us recover it," Hamilton said. His tone still seemed to imply that we knew where it was.

"To tell you the truth," I said, "I don't give a flying fuck about your diamond. The only thing I care about is finding the people who killed our friends."

There was a slight pause before he said pointedly, "Unfortunately, you may do that."

"What do you mean?"

"The Metanayans are following the trail of the diamond, and the trail leads here."

"But we don't have the diamond," Peter protested.

"All that matters is that they think you do," said Dunn.

"Why would they think that?"

"Because of your visit to a certain import-export company."

I felt the air escaping from the room. I stared at Hamilton for a moment, then I said, "Have you been following me?"

Hamilton shook his head. "There was no need to."

I stared back at him. After a moment of silence, I said, "Of course, you have someone there, don't you?"

His expression didn't change. "Things have a way of getting back to us. Especially on matters like this. You have to remember that all anybody wants is to get the diamond back to its rightful owners."

"Everybody except us, you mean."

Hamilton sighed again. "If you stand in between the Metanayans and the diamond, then your days are numbered."

"Well," Mother said stuffily, rising from her chair with a definite air of bringing the conference to a close, "thank you very much for the warning."

Hamilton and Dunn looked confused for a moment, then rose in unison.

"Mrs. Reynolds—" Hamilton began.

Mother cut him off as she ushered them to the door. "I *assure* you," she said, emphasizing the word in an imitation of Hamilton, "if we find out anything, we'll be sure to let you know."

"Mrs. Reynolds . . ." Hamilton said again, but he looked at her face and saw the steadfastness of her position. He shrugged and led Dunn through the door, which Mother closed behind them.

She paused for only a brief second, looking at the door, then wheeled around and said, "Bloody hell! What are we going to do?"

"Well, we've got to find the diamond," I replied.

"Find the diamond? Are you mad? If we had that thing our lives wouldn't be worth an hour's purchase."

"Jean," said Peter, "we're in danger whether or not we have it because they *think* we have it."

"So we'd better find it, because the only way we'll ever be safe is if we turn it in," I said.

"How on earth are we supposed to do that? It wasn't in the dolls, and I can't believe that—" She stopped, and from her expression you would have thought she'd just been kicked in the stomach.

"What?" I asked.

She eyed me warily, as if she didn't quite want to say what she was thinking. She folded her hands on her waist which gave her an aura of solemnity, and said, "I just don't know what Mason was thinking. I mean, if he took the diamond out of the doll. Do you think . . . do you think maybe he was thinking of selling it?"

"Selling it?" I repeated with distaste. "I don't think he'd do something like that. He might've been interested in what it was or how much it was worth . . . but sell it?"

Peter said, "You have to remember that he didn't know what it was. He couldn't have known it had any significance. He probably just thought it got in there by mistake, and it was his good fortune."

"Good fortune," I said wryly. I hated what they were suggesting, but I wasn't too sure it wasn't true. I loved Mason, but I didn't know whether or not he would see an unexpected windfall as a way to cash in and add to his collection. I tried not to think that he could have found out what the stone really was and held it for ransom. "But if that's true . . ." I said, thinking aloud.

"What?"

"I don't see why he didn't just take it to a jeweler to get it appraised."

"He might've done that," said Mother. "We have no way of knowing. And we can't very well canvass all the jewelers in Chicago. There're hundreds!"

"Yeah," I said feebly. My mind was still wrapped around the problem of Mason's veracity.

"Honey," said Peter, putting his arm over my shoulder, "it would've been perfectly natural to have it appraised."

"You're right," I said with a weak smile.

"But none of this gets us any forrader," said Mother, bringing us back to the matter at hand. "It doesn't matter what he was doing with it—all that matters it what he *did* with it."

This brought us to a momentary standstill while the three of us stood there in the living room looking like a trio of actors

135

who'd forgotten their lines or even whose turn it was.

Suddenly, Mother's face brightened. "Oooh, I've just had an idea."

"You know how it frightens me when you say that," I said.

"No, this isn't a dangerous one. I should go talk to Frank."

"Why?"

"Because after Ryan was killed, they're bound to have done a thorough search of the apartment. Maybe *they* found the diamond."

"I hope not," said Peter. "They don't make a lot of money."

"Oh, will you stop doing that," I said. "Not all police are criminals."

"Just a thought," Peter said with an apologetic smile. "It couldn't hurt to have them know we're in trouble."

"You're kidding," I said. I was utterly astonished that Peter would ever consent to police involvement. He'd always been the one to object before (and so had I, for that matter). But on the occasions that we'd considered calling the police we ended up not doing it until the very last minute, because to do so any earlier would have jeopardized so much. Of course, there really wasn't any reason not to call them in this time.

"You're the one who just said they're not all criminals," Peter said. "And this isn't like before. They actually might be able to help. And if all you really want to do is catch the guys who killed Mason and Ryan, we're going to have to call them in sooner or later. Why not sooner, if it can help?"

"You're the last person I would've thought would want them."

He shrugged. "Just being practical. If we want these guys put away for murder, the police are going to have to be involved. What choice do we have? I don't know about you, but I got the impression from Dunn and Hamilton that justice for Ryan and Mason was the furthest thing from their minds."

"You're right."

"I can just tell Frank what we know, and he can do whatever he thinks is best," said Mother. "Besides, if we can't find that bloody diamond, we're going to *need* the police to protect us."

"Bloody diamond is right," I said, curling my lips. "Look how many people have been killed over it."

"Well, let's just make a good job of it not being three more."

I nodded. "Well, while you do that I'm going to go and have a look around Mason and Ryan's apartment."

"Why?" said Peter. "If the police searched it, there won't be anything to find."

"Maybe not. But they weren't looking for a diamond—"

"We hope," Peter chimed in with a smile. Sometimes he just couldn't help himself.

"—so they might have overlooked it."

"I hardly think they would've missed a diamond of that size and color," Mother said, "and I don't want you going someplace where two people have already been killed. It's not safe."

"It's safer than I'd be here alone," I said. "The killers think the diamond's here, not there."

"I suppose you're right," she said reluctantly, "but I still don't like it."

"I'll come with you," Peter said.

"No, you go to work," I said. "You've already taken more time off than you should. There's no point in losing your job over this."

Peter pursed one side of his mouth—a motion he'd picked up from Mother. "There's no point in losing my job over our lives being in danger?"

I looked at him for a beat, then said, "Well, of course it sounds silly when you put it like that."

He laughed. "Besides, I can't let you have all the fun."

Mother decided that the doggie—and I cringed at the thought that she now had *me* referring to him that way, as well—would be all right left at home for a while. Then she set off for Area headquarters, where Frank was commander, and we once again headed for Mason and Ryan's apartment.

There was a curious solemnity about the two block walk. Even though Mason and Ryan were beyond caring, the thought of going through their apartment without them there was unsettling. I guess I would have felt more comfortable if at least one of them had still been around to express righteous indignation about it. Of course, if one of them had still been around, we wouldn't have been doing this.

Their not-so-humble two-flat looked positively dead, no signs of life within—not even a light left on to ward off burglars. And with the upstairs dykes gone, the building looked like a shell.

We went up to the front door and I fished in my pocket for the spare keys that we'd had so that we could water their plants while they were away. I stuck it in the lock and opened the door.

Even before switching on the lights, we could tell that something was wrong. The last time we'd been here you could still feel the heavy, intrusive presence of the police and lab techs that had tramped through the apartment. This time was different. This time it felt as if the air was stirring with chaos. And the moment we opened the door to their apartment we saw why. The living room was a shambles. I think the vibrations I had felt in the air were because nothing was in the right place. Everything had been tossed, slashed, and ruined. The beautiful couch on which we'd sat while we chatted before dinner had had its covers ripped apart and all the contents torn out and strewn on the floor. The coffee table was upended, the pictures torn from their frames and the glass smashed. Even the faux Southwestern rug was shredded. It wasn't just as if the place had been searched, it was as if the search had been performed by someone in the midst of frenzy.

After catching my breath and holding it for a moment, I suddenly started to breathe hard and fast.

"Alex," Peter said, looking at me with understandable concern. "Alex, don't."

"Look at this!" I gasped.

"Calm down! You're going to hyperventilate."

I didn't seem to be able to stop my quickened breathing until Peter wrapped his arms around me and stroked my hair, murmuring calming words in my ear.

When he finally had me composed enough so that I could breathe properly, he looked me in the face and said, "You scared me for a minute there. Don't go all to pieces on me."

"Look at this place," I said, stepping past him. My shock had been replaced by a sick feeling in the stomach. "Look what they did!"

"Jean was right—the place has already been searched."

"The police didn't do this!"

"I know," Peter replied, laying a hand on my shoulder.

"They've gone through this place like a tornado. If the diamond was here, they found it."

"And they didn't find it, or they wouldn't have been searching our house."

I turned to him. "We still don't know that it was those Metanayan people who were in the house."

Peter smiled. "You're beginning to sound like me."

"I wish I hadn't been so stupid and we'd gotten a look at who it was," I said with a stamp of my right foot.

"It's no use going over that."

We stood for a few moments in silence, both of us transfixed by the mess that was once a minor showplace. Mason would have been sick if he'd seen this.

"How could they have done all this without being heard?" I said.

"There was nobody here to hear them. Linda and Ronnie moved out, remember?"

"It looks like it was a good thing they did. I don't like to think what might've happened if someone had been nearby when this happened."

After a pause, Peter said, "Well, what are we going to do now?"

I searched my brain for a couple of minutes, trying to find some glimmer of an idea for how we should proceed. None of the parties concerned had given us much to go on, and now that we knew our lives were in danger, it was vital that we sort this mess out. But where to start?

Suddenly, a thought hit me. "Wait. Didn't we go to a Buddhist church once?"

"I don't think anyone's ever been to a Buddhist *church*."

"I mean temple, or whatever they call it. Didn't we visit one once?"

"I don't . . ." He had that "you've slipped a cog" look on his face that he manages to make so attractive. Suddenly his expression brightened. "Oh, yeah, I remember. During the Old Town Art Fair."

"Yeah. It was open and we stopped and visited."

"Uh-huh," he said warily. It was the first time I realized that Peter was beginning to respond to me when I had the dawnings of a new idea the same way I respond to Mother when she does it. Somewhere in the back of my mind I wondered if the Reynolds clan carried some sort of Lucy-link in their genes.

"Why don't we go there and talk to them—him—whoever's in charge."

"For what?"

"Well, I've never heard of Metanayans before now, have you?"

"No."

"If they really are some sort of bizarre offshoot of Buddhists, wouldn't you think a Buddhist official would know about them?"

"A Buddhist official?" Peter repeated in a tone that I'm sure he didn't mean to make me feel as foolish as I did.

"Whatever they're called. They should know about the Metanayans, shouldn't they?"

"So what?"

"So . . . if we can't find that goddamn diamond then we're going to have to find those goddamn people that're after it and try to convince them that we don't have it!"

"We don't have to find them, sweetheart, they're looking for us."

"I have a feeling they already know where we are, but any way you look at it, I think it would look better if we were looking for them."

Peter stared at me for a moment, then said, "You know, that almost makes sense."

"Almost!" I exclaimed, giving him a semi-playful slap on the shoulder. "It makes perfect sense to me."

He gave me a light kiss on the lips, drew back, and said, "I know."

At least he smiled when he said it.

ELEVEN

We had the cab drop us off at Clark Street and Webster because I thought I remembered the temple as being somewhere on Webster. In case I was wrong, we didn't want to have the cab driver roam the streets looking for the temple when we could just as easily cover the ground on foot. Fortunately my memory hadn't failed me, and we found the place just two blocks west of Clark.

The temple was in the center of the block. It was a tiny building done in pseudo-oriental style, although it was only the location that made it seem unreal. Given its purpose, I suppose the architecture was authentic. It was set in the middle of a garden of stunted plants and trees that I figured must be awfully hard to maintain in the Chicago weather. But patience is a Buddhist thing. At least I think it is. The grounds were surrounded by a wide-set iron fence about five feet tall, with a small plaque on the gate that said LHASA BUDDHIST TEMPLE.

The building itself was a mixture of red and black and gold. We went through the gate and up the front walk, then up the wooden stairs to the front door. Peter gave me a sidelong glance that seemed to say he couldn't believe we were doing this, which was all the encouragement I needed to push open the door with added purpose and walk in.

Inside there was a lobby (or whatever they call it) barely three yards wide, and beyond that a vast room (I have no idea what they call that either), the focal point of which was an elaborate gold altar with a statue of Buddha that—even sitting down—was taller than me. There was nothing in its navel, which either meant that these were the type of Buddhists I've always read about, who eschew worldly possessions, or it was open season on forty-carat navel lint.

On a mat on the floor in front of the Buddha was a man who looked like he was wearing white cotton pajamas. He was sitting in the lotus position with his hands folded in his lap so that his fingers and thumbs formed an O. I had this sudden flashback to the seventies: beds with no frames, black posters on the walls, black lights on the floor, and smoking weed while listening to Rod McKuen read *Jonathan Livingston Seagull*. God, Mother was tolerant.

"What should we do?" I whispered to Peter. I wasn't happy to find my whisper echoing in the room.

"We can't interrupt him," Peter replied. "It would be rude."

"We can't stay here all day waiting for him to finish meditating . . . or praying . . . or whatever he's doing. They can do that for hours, can't they?"

"I don't know. I don't know enough about it. But I'm still not going to interrupt him."

"Yes," said a pleasant, subdued voice, "a disciplined Buddhist is more than able to meditate for hours at a time."

Despite the serenity of the voice, both Peter and I jumped when we heard it. While we'd been holding our whispered tête à tête, the man had managed to materialize at our side. He was an Asian gentleman, about a foot shorter than me, and his upturned face held the most peaceful expression I've ever seen anywhere. I looked back to where he'd been sitting. I couldn't imagine how he'd gotten up to us without being heard. It gave me the creeps.

"I'm terribly sorry that we disturbed you," said Peter, always first to remember his manners.

"You have not disturbed me," the man replied. He didn't look as if anything could ever do that.

"Are you in charge here?" I asked.

He turned that beaming face to me. "Who can say?"

I glanced at Peter. "Well, you can, can't you? I mean . . ."

"I know what you mean," the man replied with a gentle smile. "I suppose you can say that I'm in charge at the moment."

I glanced at Peter again. He looked amused. But I was just frustrated. This wasn't exactly the kind of response that inspired confidence. But since there was nobody else there, we didn't have much of a choice.

"Could we ask you a couple of questions?" I said.

He bowed his head slightly and replied, "I will answer them if I am able."

"What do you know . . . Have you ever heard of the Metanayans?"

For a split second the man's serene visage froze like a photograph. I had apparently troubled his tranquility. I wondered if he was going to have to do extra meditating for that.

"I have heard of them, yes," he said with no enthusiasm.

Peter looked at me, then back at the man. He took a deep breath and the reins at the same time. "We thought maybe, since you are a Buddhist, that you might be able to tell us something about them."

"What did you wish to know?"

"Well, for one thing, where we can find them?" I said.

"Why would you wish to do that?"

I was beginning to feel like a mouse trapped between the playful paws of a cat. A gentle, smiling cat.

"For reasons of our own," Peter said much more gracefully than I could have.

"Well," said the man, flashing a knowing grin at Peter, "I'm afraid that you wouldn't find any here in Chicago. The only Metanayan group that I know of in the United States is in the District of Columbia."

"So . . . if there were some Metanayans here at the moment,

they would be from Washington?" I asked.

The man turned his curious eyes toward me. "I've heard nothing of them establishing themselves here. I think I would have. So you are very correct. I would think they would be . . . visiting from somewhere else." He tilted his head slightly. "I wonder what they would be here for?"

"They've come here looking for something that belongs to them," said Peter.

"Really?" said the man, turning to him. "What would that be?" I couldn't swear to it, but in the brief interval before he averted his face from me, I could've sworn there'd been some sort of recognition there, as if he already knew the answer to his own question. It made me wonder if perhaps the head of the temple had been told to keep his eyes open for the icon.

Peter could easily see me over the man's head. I shook my head at him.

"We don't really know," he said to the man, "but they seem to think we have it."

The man shook his head and clucked his tongue sadly. "This is very bad. The Metanayans, unlike Buddhists, are not known to be patient. It is unwise, if one desires to stay alive on this earthly plane, to run afoul of them."

"I don't understand," I said. "If these people are an offshoot of Buddhism, how can they be violent?"

"There are those everywhere," he said benignly, "who believe that peace, whether it is peace of the heart, or peace of the mind, or peace in the world, can be achieved by violence. They are blinded to the folly of such beliefs, because the reality is that violence only begets violence. I think it very unwise of you to try to find them."

"But we have to," I said.

"There is nothing that really has to be done, other than meditation," he said with a shrug. If he was trying to warn us off, he had certainly chosen a peculiar way to do it.

"If we want to stay alive, we have to," Peter said.

The man turned to Peter and said, "Why?" It was such a direct question that it almost startled me.

"Because we have to explain to them that we *don't* have what they're looking for. They've somehow gotten the idea that we do."

"They must have some reason for believing it," the man said after a slight pause. There followed a silence that was curiously tense for someone who was supposed to be serene. This guy seemed to be challenging us. I got the feeling that like everybody else he thought we had the damn thing. It reinforced the idea that he already knew about the whole mess and was told to be on the lookout.

"But we don't have it," I said firmly.

The man sighed with disappointment, then said, "If that is true, then I pity you and envy you."

"Why?" I asked.

"Because the Metanayans, whatever other beliefs they may hold, are trained in meditation. They have a definite advantage over most Americans."

"What's that?"

He smiled broadly. "Focus. Like most who meditate regularly they are capable of remaining focused in a way that most Americans would find impossible to achieve. They are too busy running helter-skelter among the cares and worries of the world."

"And the focus is on us," said Peter.

"So you say," the man replied with another bow of his head. "And ordinarily they would not focus on anything without reason."

He looked up at me and blinked. Those peaceful eyes seemed to be piercing into my head.

"We really don't have the thing!" I exclaimed, shaking my head to loosen his gaze from it.

"That is a pity," he said. "Then I am afraid there is nothing I can do to help you."

Both Peter and I were quick to catch the implications of this, but Peter was the one who spoke. "You mean that if we had the thing, you could help us?"

"I mean if you had it, you could help yourselves. Without it,

146

I do not know what you can do. The Metanayans are sure to remain intent on their object until they are sure that that object may not be obtained through you."

Peter looked at me and cocked his head toward the door. I looked down at the man, and realized after a few seconds that my mouth was hanging open. If what he was telling us was true, we were in big sheep dip.

We started to walk away from him, but I stopped suddenly and turned back. "Oh. What was the other thing?"

"I beg your pardon?" he replied.

"You said that you pitied us an envied us. You told us why you pitied us, but why the hell would you envy us?"

His smile was once again very broad, but his eyes were not happy.

"Because you will surely achieve Nirvana before I do."

"But I don't want to achieve Nirvana," I whined as we hurried back to Clark Street to find a cab.

"Especially not the way he thinks we're going to do it," Peter said pointedly.

"He made it sound like a threat. Buddhists aren't supposed to do that, are they?"

"I don't know. You've seen Richard Gere movies. He always looks like a loose cannon."

As usual, there was a steady stream of cabs on Clark Street, and we flagged the first one that was empty and sped back to our humble townhouse on Fullerton. Neither of us had much to say on the way there, mainly due to the fact that we were at a loss for what to do next. I don't know what was going on in Peter's head, but my own mind was jumble of diamonds and sinister-looking people popping up behind our garage and flashlights in the dark and assorted things that had already happened, but none of it gelled into a plan for the future. The worst part about it was that with these people popping up everywhere, including inside our house, I was beginning to feel like we weren't safe anywhere. And if the Buddhist priest or monk or whatever he was had been telling the truth (and I thought they had to be truthful), then I was right.

When we got back to the house it was a minute or two before I remembered to be surprised that the dog hadn't run up to greet me with that helicopter-blade–like tail of his: mainly because I kept forgetting that we had him. I plopped down on the couch and Peter said he was going to get a Coke from the refrigerator and asked me if I wanted one. I said yes and he headed for the kitchen.

It was then that I heard a muffled whimper from beneath the couch. I slid to my knees and looked under it, and there were those two bulgy eyes looking back at me, and the perpetually perky ears standing up at attention. His tail wasn't wagging.

"What are you doing under there?" I asked as if he could answer me. "Come on out."

He crawled out under the low board that crossed the length of the couch, then stood up, looking at me pleadingly.

"What the hell is wrong with you?" I said lightly. "Why were you hiding under the couch? And why are you looking like that?"

His attention was suddenly caught by something behind me, and I turned to see what it was just as an arm caught me around the throat. Before I knew what was happening, I was spun around and slammed against the wall, my neck in the clutch of a tight grip. Instinctively my hands flew up to my neck to try to wrench the hand away, but I was stopped almost immediately.

There were two of them, and it didn't take much imagination to figure out that they must be the Metanayans we'd been hearing so much about. But it wasn't the sight of them that had stopped me from struggling, it was the sight of the knife. The first man was holding my throat with his left hand, and in his right he held a large, curved ceremonial knife that came to a very nasty-looking point. That point was not necessarily needed, however, because the actual blade of the knife looked like it could split each individual hair on my head—not to mention my head.

The biggest surprise was the way they looked. I suppose I expected them to look like the leering Oriental bad guys of movies of the thirties and forties. Instead they were dressed as respectably as Linda had described them. Both were in expensive-looking gray suits, white shirts, and dark ties. They looked like businessmen with an attitude.

I frantically tried to choke out some words. "Where's . . . where's Peter? Where is he?"

"Where is the stone?" said the one holding my neck.

"The stone?"

He shoved upward with his hand, raising my chin and knocking my head back against the wall. His grip tightened slightly.

"You know what I'm talking about! Where's the Stone of the Buddha?"

Christ, I thought, *I wish people would stop saying things like that to me. It makes me want to giggle.*

"I know . . ." I struggled to talk through my constricted throat. "I know you won't believe it . . . but I don't have it. I really don't have it. I . . ."

He tightened his grip a little more.

"You have been trying to find out its worth. I can tell you what it is worth. It is worth your life."

Despite the way he was holding me and the threat his words implied, he looked and sounded calm enough to be chairing a meeting at General Motors.

"We haven't been trying to find out what it's worth! We've been trying to find out what it *is,* so that we can find the damn thing and return it to you!"

He placed the point of the knife about half an inch under my right eye and slowly, lightly traced an arc beneath it. His level of composure was scaring me to death. That and the business suit. I think it would have been less unnerving if he'd been in a black mask and cowl, but the incongruity of having someone who looked like an advertising executive brandishing a ceremonial knife at me somehow made him seem more dangerous.

"You are lying," he said. "You know where the Stone of the Buddha is."

"We only just found out *what* it is," I explained desperately, "but we don't know where it is. You have to believe me! We've been trying to find it, too!"

His grip tightened just a bit more. He must have been really well trained in this sort of thing, because despite the fact that I felt like I couldn't breathe, I was getting enough oxygen to keep me from passing out.

"I could squeeze the life out of you, but that wouldn't be fun. What I would like to do instead is to cut it out."

For the first time, I felt the strength of my hatred for these two guys surging up in me. I managed to say, "Like you did to my friends?"

"Exactly," he said. His smile was so unaffected that I could feel my blood turning cold. I almost shivered.

Without warning, he pulled me forward with the hand holding my neck and tossed me in the direction of his friend, who grabbed my arms and twisted them behind my back. He caught both of my wrists together in a viselike grip with one hand and wrapped his other arm around my neck.

The man with the knife advanced and gently tugged at the top button of my shirt.

"I wonder," he said, slicing the button off with one smooth move. As he continued to speak, he cut off each of the remaining buttons for punctuation. "I wonder if you will make the same noises as your friends did when I gutted them. Will you try to cry out? But nobody will hear you, will they? My partner will see to that."

"But they didn't know anything!" I said, trying to yell it at them but unable to because of the arm across my throat. "They didn't know anything! You killed them for nothing, and it'll be the same thing if you kill me. I don't know where the diamond is!"

He had cut off all the buttons and slowly pulled my shirt open. Then he placed the flat of the blade on my stomach, slowly running its edge upward as he continued. "Or maybe you're trying to get money from us for the return of the stone. I wouldn't advise it."

It flashed through my mind that with Mother's money and

what Peter and I bring in from selling clothes, freelance artwork, and spying, money was the last thing we needed. The confusion I felt at his suggestion must've registered on my face, and he took that as confirmation.

"Ah!" he said, raising the knife to my face, "I see it's true. You have made a very bad mistake. We will get what we want. I will peel your little family apart one by one until you tell me what I want to know. And I promise you, you will tell me. . . ."

For the second time that day I had a flashback. It was to when I told Mother that I was gay. I don't know what kind of response I expected, but after blinking at me once, she said, "Well, if you're going to be gay then I'm going to have to teach you about men. There are two things you have to remember: Never sleep with one on the first date, and a well-placed knee can solve many a sticky situation."

He was just drawing the knife away from my face—to do what, I don't even want to know—when I surged forward and brought my knee into contact with his groin as solidly as I knew how. There was a startled look on his face for one split second before he doubled over in pain with a high pitched yowl. My lunge had thrown the guy holding me off balance enough that his hold on my arms loosened. I wrenched my right arm free and brought my elbow back into his ribs.

He wasn't quite so easy to shake, though. Even though he bent slightly with the blow, he still managed to keep hold of my left arm. He tried to twist me around to face him but was in enough pain that he didn't seem to be able to manage a maneuver that I was trying to make as complicated as possible. I was struggling as hard as I could to twist myself out of his grasp. Fortunately, in doing this I managed to get him to step backward and he tripped very unexpectedly over his fallen friend. It was good that it was unexpected because he was caught so off-guard that he instantly let go of me as he toppled wildly backward, striking his head against the dining table.

The minute I was free I took off like a madman for the front door, and was almost there when I heard a faint *whoosh* and found my right leg stuck in place. I pulled frantically at it, and turned to see what had happened.

The first assailant, the one who'd been doubled up on the floor, had managed to get enough strength back to take a swipe at my retreating form with the knife. He managed to catch the hem of my pants and part of the heel of my shoe with the point of the knife, pinning them (and me) to the floor just a few feet from the front door. He pulled himself up as best he could. He was still in enough pain that he couldn't straighten up completely. Now he actually did look like those maniacal bad guys from the movies.

I tried to get free of the knife, and probably could have if the damn thing hadn't caught my shoe, too. But it didn't matter, because he was on me before I could really do anything. Again his arm went around my throat, but instead of any sort of threat, there was a surreal pause before the whole room seemed to spin with stars, planets, and small gift-wrapped boxes. It was a few seconds before the pain registered, and I realized he had struck a savage blow to one of my kidneys. The only fortunate thing about it was that he used his fist.

But while I was doubled over, he pulled the knife out of the floor. He then grabbed me by the hair and pulled my head back.

It was at that moment that Mother walked through the door, calling out "Alex, I'm home and—"

"Mother! Run! Get out!" I cried out.

But it was too late. She stopped in her tracks just inside the door. Her eyes widened to saucers and she said, "Jiminy Christmas!"

"Don't move," said the man holding me. "Do exactly as I say, or your son will die immediately."

He took a couple of steps back, pulling me along with him.

"Come in. I believe you are Mrs. Reynolds, aren't you? Come in. Join us."

Mother's eyes were wide, but for some reason she didn't seem particularly surprised: probably because the past couple of years our lives have tended to scenes like this. I suppose she wouldn't be surprised if she came home and found me cavorting naked with a Spanish circus. She took a couple of steps forward, then stopped.

"Now, what shall we do?" said the man holding me. I could feel his hot breath on my neck and the sinister smile in his voice. All the while he kept the knife curved around my throat.

"Drop it!" Commander Frank O'Neil stepped into the doorway with his gun drawn and pointed at my captor, although it looked as if the gun was aimed at my face. Despite that, I'd never been so happy to see a gun in my life. Frank stepped around mother, shielding her and waving her back. He probably wanted her to get out of the house, but if he actually thought she would do it, he didn't know her very well.

"Drop it," he repeated firmly.

"He'll be dead before the bullet hits me," said the man.

"I wouldn't count on it," said Frank. "You so much as scratch that boy and you'll be dead before he hits the floor."

I didn't know whether I was more offended at being referred to as a boy, or by the fact that my fate didn't seem to matter to either of them.

There was a tense pause during which time seemed to stand still while my mind raced through everything I'd ever done wrong in my lifetime. I didn't think for a minute that this guy would shrink from killing me, and under the circumstances there wasn't very much comfort in knowing that if he did, he'd be caught. Suddenly, an idea flashed through my mind.

"If you kill me," I choked the words out, "you'll *never* find it."

There was a barely noticeable loosening of the grip around my neck. The man's breathing quickened. There was a pause that seemed to last an eternity, then suddenly I saw Frank and Mother hurtling toward me. It wasn't until the impact that I realized that the man holding me had simply shoved me into them. Mother managed to leap out of the way as I crashed into Frank, the impact throwing the both of us back into the wall by the front door. I tumbled to the floor, bringing Frank with me.

"Get off me!" Frank exclaimed, rolling my inert body over and scrambling to his feet.

But it had been enough time for the two men to beat a hasty retreat through the back door. Frank got to his feet and lit out after them, and Mother helped me up.

"Are you all right?" she said. Her voice was strained and her eyes full of concern.

I straightened myself up and was about to answer her when suddenly I remembered that Peter had gone into the kitchen and never come back. "Oh, Christ!" I said loudly as I ran to the kitchen.

Peter lay crumpled into a ball on the tiles. He was moaning softly and with his right hand was feeling the back of his head.

"Are you all right? Peter? Say something!"

He rolled over on his back and looked surprised to find Mother and me standing over him, looking down at him with frantic faces.

"What hit me?" he asked weakly.

"A Metanayan," I said, pulling him up to his feet. "I don't know what he hit you with."

"Jesus, my head hurts!"

"You're lucky that's all that hurts," I said. "They were planning to do the same thing to the three of us that they did to Mason and Ryan."

"What?" Mother said indignantly. "Here? In this house?" She sounded as if she was more affronted by the fact that our two would-be assailants were going to create a mess in her home than by the fact that they were going to kill us.

Further discussion was interrupted by Frank returning from the chase. He brushed the hair back out of his face and holstered his gun. "Not a sign of them. They must've disappeared into thin air the minute they were out of this house. Great. Now I have to find two Asians in Chicago. That'll be a trick!"

"I don't think they're from Chicago," I said. "I think they're from Washington. They must be staying here somewhere."

"Oh, even better! I have to find two Asian *tourists* in Chicago! That'll be even easier!"

"I need to sit down," Peter said, wincing as he touched the back of his head.

"I'll get you a cloth," said Mother.

We sat at the kitchen table, and Mother ran a towel under the faucet and then stood behind Peter and pressed it to his head. He flinched at first contact, but then it seemed to soothe him a bit.

"How did you happen to come home with Mother?" I asked Frank.

Before answering he shot Mother a glance that spoke volumes. Frank and Mother had dated at one time, and though Mother had broken it off, Frank had always shown signs of still carrying a little torch for her. Well, actually, a pretty big torch. Mother, on the hand, with her heritage of British loyalty, had insisted on maintaining a friendship with him even though it probably would have been wiser to not have anything to do with him at all. In the past when we'd gotten in trouble we'd had to keep him in the dark—a fact that he deeply resented. I think he somehow retained the hope that he could win her back, and finding out that we'd been in trouble and gotten out of it ourselves robbed him of his chance to play Lancelot to her Guinevere. Ah, love.

"When Jean told me what you were up to this time—and I'm sure glad I'm hearing about it almost at the start—I told her I thought I'd better talk to you myself."

"Why?" I said, wondering if I looked as wild-eyed as I felt. What had just happened was finally beginning to sink in. "Mother would have told you everything I could."

"I want to hear it straight from you, start to finish."

I took a deep breath and told him everything that we'd learned since Mason and Ryan had been killed, including the home invasion of the previous night and the mysterious accountant-like guy who appeared behind our garage right afterward. I then explained that according to a Buddhist priest—or whatever they're called—our antagonists had apparently come from Washington.

"You didn't recognize either of these guys?" he said when I finished.

"No."

"I mean, the two guys that were here tonight. Was either of them the one behind the garage?"

I shook my head. "No. The one behind the garage was at the Thai import company, that's all I know about him."

"You don't have any idea where this diamond is?" Frank said skeptically.

"We thought *you* had it," said Peter, wincing slightly.

Frank looked at him. "No. We didn't find anything of value in their apartment." He then turned to me and said, "Are you *sure* you don't have the diamond?"

"Look, I know we haven't always been up front with you, but I'm telling you the truth! We don't know where the fucking thing is!"

"Alex . . ." Mother said, presumably objecting to the expletive.

"Don't you think we'd just give it to them if we had it?"

Frank tilted his head sideways and narrowed his eyes at me. "I suppose so."

"You *suppose* so? What do you think we are, crazy?"

Mother cleared her throat.

"We don't *want* to be cut apart, for Chrissakes!"

Peter reached over and put his hand gently over mine. "Honey, you're making my head hurt."

"Sorry," I said sheepishly.

There was a beat before Frank said, "So, these guys are after you for the diamond, and you don't have it. That's bad."

"That's not the point, Frank! Those two men who were just here are the guys that killed Mason and Ryan! They told me that much! We've got to catch them and bring them to justice!"

Frank looked at me for a few moments, then said, "We?"

"All right, *you!* I don't care who does it as long as they pay for what they've done."

Frank leaned back in his chair and sighed. "Okay. First, we're going to have to put your house under surveillance. If what you tell me is true, and they're not going to stop until they get that diamond back, then you're in danger and we're going to have to protect you."

Surprisingly enough, neither Peter nor Mother objected. I half expected Peter to object, because he had in the past. But that was when we were dealing with spies who somehow seemed rational in comparison with what we were dealing with now.

"Yes. Now we're in even more danger than we were before," said Mother, eyeing me significantly.

"How could we possibly be?" I asked.

"Because you just told them we *have* the diamond. You said if they killed you they'd never get it back."

My jaw dropped. "But I just said that to keep him from killing me."

"I understand that, but now they're convinced that we have it."

I blinked at her, then said, "Oh, dear God!" I lowered my head to the table with a thud and put my hands on top of my head.

"Exactly, darling," said Mother, "and we'd better hope dear God is looking out for us because we're surely in the soup now."

After a few moments of silence during which I wondered who would handle the funerals if all three of us were killed at the same time, I raised my head, looked at Frank, and said, "You're not going to have to watch the house."

"What?" Frank said in disbelief.

"Because we're not going to be here."

"Where are we going?" said Mother.

"It's way too dangerous for us to stay here. We've got to get out of town."

Mother looked at me with raised eyebrows. Apparently she was surprised that I would think of running. From the look on Peter's face he had just experienced another stab of pain, so it was impossible to tell what he was thinking.

Frank stared at me for a moment, then looked at Mother. He looked as if he were disappointed that once again he would be robbed of the opportunity to save her from the bad guys, but he couldn't hide the fact that he thought getting out of town was a good idea. He pushed back his chair and got up as he said to me, "That's probably the best thing to do. When will you leave?"

"In the morning," I said, "as early as possible."

He looked down at me. "Not as early as possible. First, you're going to have to go with me to that Thai import company and identify the guy that was behind the garage."

"Why? He wasn't one of the attackers. If anything, he was trying to help us . . . or at least warn us."

"It's too suspicious that he turned up here at the same time as your house getting broken into."

I'm embarrassed to say that I hadn't thought of that, although I found the guy suspicious enough in his own right.

"If he isn't in on this," Frank continued, "then he probably knows something about it. It can't be a coincidence that these Meta-whatsits were able to find you right after you went to that company. Somebody had to tell them who you were."

"But it could've been anybody there," I said. "There were an awful lot of people in that office."

"Still couldn't hurt to question him," Frank said with a shrug. "And I'm still going to have to arrange surveillance for tonight." He turned to Mother and added, "Can I use the phone?"

"Certainly," she replied. "Use the one in the living room."

Once Frank had passed through the doorway between the kitchen and the dining area, Mother pushed the swinging door closed.

"What are you thinking?"

"Just what I said. We've got to get out of here."

"And go where?" Peter asked.

"To Washington."

"Huh?"

"Look, we don't have the damn diamond, so if we're going to get out of this alive we have two choices: We can either find the diamond and give it back to them, or we can find the head of this merry little clan and try to convince him that we don't have it! And since we don't even know where to begin looking for the diamond—every place it could be has been turned inside out—then I think the second option is our only hope."

"I don't know," said Mother, wrinkling her nose. "It doesn't sound as if they're any too easy to convince."

"But all we've seen are the people who were sent to get the thing back no matter what. There's got to be somebody in their group that's . . . well, sane!"

"I wouldn't count on it, darling. They sound all of a pin."

Peter turned his pain-contorted face to her, and my own expression probably mirrored his.

"What?" I said.

"All of a pin. All the same. Just like pins," she explained with a shrug, looking exactly as if she thought we were both slow.

"You know, I hate to say it, but Frank might be right," Peter said.

"About what?"

"The guy behind the garage. Maybe he was just sent to feel us out—to see if we had the diamond and convince us that we'd better give it back without any trouble."

I drew myself up in my chair, probably looking much as Mother does when she "gets her back up." "They bought trouble when they killed Mason and Ryan."

Despite the seriousness of the situation, there was a look in Peter's eyes that showed me he was proud of me. Mother had the same expression, only she managed to look worried at the same time.

"We're in agreement about that," said Peter. "But why don't we just see if Dunn and Hamilton can convince these people that we don't have the diamond? Hell, they're with the State Department, aren't they? That's part of their job."

"We told them we didn't have it, and they didn't seem to believe us. But there's one person who would believe us—at least he knows us well enough to believe us."

Peter nodded. "Agent Lawrence Nelson. But we could just call him."

I shook my head briskly. "We might as well go and see him. We're in far too much danger here."

"Well," said Mother, heaving a sigh, "if we're going on a trip I'll have to make arrangements for the doggie."

"Are you going to leave him with Mattie?" I asked hopefully.

"Good Heavens, no! I wouldn't leave Duffy with a stranger. I'm going to get a carrier so I can bring him with us!"

This time *I* groaned.

TWELVE

The rest of the day was pretty much a mad dash to get all the arrangements made for our unexpected trip. But first we took Peter to the doctor to have his head checked. When the doctor asked how Peter had received his injury, we couldn't exactly explain to him that Peter had been conked on the head by a raging Metanayan. Mother used her disquieting talent for extemporation and came up with a story about how Peter had slipped on an egg that she'd just dropped on the floor and hit his head on the corner of the stove on his way down.

Doctor Jamison, a wizened young man of about forty who'd been our family doctor for about five years, blinked at her through his heavy glasses. I got the impression that he didn't believe her—after all, he had to know the dent in Peter's head didn't fit the story—but he didn't bother pursuing the matter. He merely told us what the signs of concussion were, and that if Peter showed any of them we were to call him right away. After the visit with the doctor we make a quick swing by the Park View Pet Shop for a carrier for the dog.

All through these little errands we were followed at an indiscreet distance by one of Frank's men in an unmarked car. He didn't bother trying to stay out of sight because there was no reason to disguise his presence from us, and his high visibility was probably an asset to us at that point.

Later that evening, I found I was having a delayed reaction to the attack. I'd gotten beyond fear for myself and moved on to being so worried about Peter that I became oversolicitous enough to get him annoyed. When we got home and I offered to get him some tea, he waved me away—in an offhand manner that would've made *me* crack him on the head if someone hadn't already done it for me—and said he would get it himself.

Mother waved us both off and said she'd make it, because after all she was British and what the 'ell did *we* know about making tea. Peter laughed and held his head.

"Sometimes I wonder if she's aware that she's the one from another country," he said.

After tea I made reservations for the earliest flight I could get us on and still have time to go with Frank to the import company.

I don't think any of us slept that night, despite the honor guard that sat outside our house. Just for the record, when one is being pursued by foreign assassins, it really does make you feel more secure to know that the police are watching your house— no matter how you might feel about a police state.

The next morning I went with Frank to the Thai Import/Export Company of Chicago. It was a wasted trip, as I knew it would be. The man who'd cornered me behind the garage wasn't there, and neither were the two assailants—and I swear to God the rest of them were *trying* to look alike just to make me look like a fool. Along with Mr. Sukin, all of the employees seemed to be conspiring to pull one of those routines out of *The Lady Vanishes*, either denying any knowledge of the man we were looking for, or pretending they didn't speak English and couldn't understand us. If this sounds at all prejudicial, you have to remember that I was under a lot of stress by that point—what with two friends dead and having been threatened with seeing the insides of my own stomach. I'm sure the ones who said they couldn't understand us probably really couldn't.

Less than two hours later, Mother, Peter, and I (along with the dog) were on a plane to Washington, D.C. All the way to the airport I kept a sharp eye out the back window, trying to tell whether or not we were being followed. The police guard kept close on our tail, but I couldn't tell if there was anybody behind them because the traffic was so heavy and so slow that it looked like we were being shadowed by everyone.

On the plane, Peter and I sat on one side of the aisle, and Mother sat in the window seat on the other with the dog belted into the seat on the aisle.

"How's your head?" I said to Peter.

"Are you going to ask me that every half hour?"

I nodded. "Until the welt goes away, yes."

He leaned over and whispered lovingly into my ear, "No dizziness. No nausea. The only fluttering in my stomach is when I look at you and those beautiful blue eyes of yours. I still get butterflies."

I drew back slightly from him, smiled, and said, "If you think that's going to get me off your case, you're out of your mind."

He laughed, leaned over, and kissed me lightly on my earlobe. I happened to look up at that moment, and the flight attendant— a young guy who looked like he'd stepped out of a Colt video and into his uniform—noticed us, smiled and gave us a wink. I found myself humming "We Are Family."

When we were coming into Washington, I saw at once that Mason had been right. There is something stirring and majestic about all the memorials, monuments, and huge, ornate government buildings that makes even a little faggot's heart swell with pride. Just coming in for a landing in Washington gave me the feeling that I was entering the seat of the civilized world. Then again, I feel that way every time Peter and I make love.

Once we'd landed, we had to find some way to get to the hotel.

"We'll get a taxi," said Mother.

"Why don't we just rent a car?" I said.

Mother turned to me, her expression absolutely dumbfounded: "Honestly, Alex, sometimes I wonder who raised you."

"What?"

"You act like you've never been followed by killers before. Where is your head on this case!"

"I haven't seen hide nor hair of those Metanayan people since we left home this morning."

"They didn't have to follow us here," Mother explained patiently, "they only had to find out where we were going. Then all they had to do was call their people here and have them pick up on us."

"But we *want* to talk to them," I said.

"Huh! We bloody well better talk to them on our terms, and that means finding them before they find us."

Mother had, in fact, decided we should take a cab because it would be much harder to follow. In that she proved correct. We have a helluva lot of cabs in Chicago, but we pale in comparison to the veritable sea of taxis and limos that were on the streets of our nation's capital. They were all performing some sort of demonic bumper car race, weaving in and out and around us. It was as if all of their occupants had screamed "I'm being followed—lose him!" as they leapt into the various vehicles. And the sheer number of cabs was mind-boggling. I really believe we'd gone over a mile before I saw an actual car.

Our destination was the Georgetown Suites on Thirty-first just off M Street. The minute I saw the sign for M Street I pointed it out to Peter and Mother.

"Just like the Peter Lorre movie," I said. "And pretty apt."

"M for murderer," Peter said, nodding.

"Don't be so portentous, darlings," said Mother as she rubbed the dog's snout with her index finger through the wire gate of its carrier. "If our luck holds out, we'll be able to take care of everything with nary a one of us being murdered."

We pulled up in front of the hotel, which was huge and elegant. The only excuse for this expense was that Mother likes luxury. I do, too, but I have the decency to feel a little guilty about indulging in it. I suppose that stems from the fact that in my early childhood I heard echoes of the admonition that children should clean their plates because people were starving in Europe. Mother, however, was in Europe (or at least England, because like any good Brit she will never refer to England as being part of Europe) while people were supposed to be starving there, and she's always said that "want" and "plenty" should be enjoyed in equal measures.

Anyway, the hotel was enormous and painted bright white, with a short marble staircase leading up to massive glass doors that were opened for us by twin doormen. I mean that literally. The interior went over the edge of posh into the land of conspicuous opulence. Obvious expense was everywhere, from the filigree frames of the portraits of the presidents across one wall of the lobby, to the plush, red-carpeted staircase that I swear was from the set of *Gone with the Wind*. Men in Italian suits strolled by with a self-possession that let you know they were in no hurry to get where they were going, because nothing important would be done until they got there. The women were adorned with modest diamonds proper to the time of day—I imagined they would all look like chandeliers by nightfall—and business suits or dresses depending on whether they were attending meetings or luncheons.

And then there were the three of us. Dressed like normal American citizens. When we went to check in, the desk clerk was so haughty toward us that I could feel frost forming on my nose. And the look she gave the dog when Mother set its carrier on the desk was enough to make me want to snatch the animal up in my arms and hug it protectively. At least, that was the clerk's attitude until she asked how we would be paying, and Mother pulled a wallet from her purse, opened it, and made a point of accidently spilling a half-dozen Platinum Cards on the counter. She gave an apologetic half-smile to the clerk, glanced at the cards and with a show of absentmindedness that could've won her an

Oscar on the opposite coast, picked a card at random, handed it to the clerk and said, "Oh, use this one, I guess." She then gathered up the rest like a bridge deck, shuffled them and slipped them back into her wallet.

We were shown to our neighboring rooms by a pair of bellmen who looked like they couldn't decide whether to pay more attention to Mother, where the money was, or to Peter, who could turn heads in a monastery. I trailed behind, rolling my eyes like Laura Petrie.

The suite into which Peter and I found ourselves ushered was a study in tasteful elegance. There was a living room complete with sitting area, an entertainment center and wet bar, and the bedroom was so posh it made me want to set aside our present troubles—dire as they were—and spend the afternoon naked in bed with Peter and a box of chocolates.

The bellman opened the curtains and said to Peter, "That's the Potomac."

"Very nice," I said with a slight edge in my voice as I stepped between the two of them and looked out the window. Peter smiled.

"If you need anything," the bellman continued, still paying particular attention to Peter, "anything at all, please don't hesitate to call. I'll be glad to do anything."

"We will," said Peter, emphasizing the *we*. He then handed the kid a tip that was healthy enough to make me blink. The bellman smiled and left at a leisurely pace.

"Hmm," I said.

"What?" Peter was trying hard to look innocent.

"That was the first time I've ever seen the chickenhawk routine in reverse."

He smiled, put his hands on my waist, and drew me closer. "Are you calling me old?"

"Of course not," I said, breaking into a smile. "Even uneducated bellmen know that you're just right."

He reached up and ran his fingers through my hair, then

166

rested his hand at the back of my head.

"Did you see the bedroom?" he asked softly.

"All that's missing is scantily-clad slave boys stirring the air with palm fronds."

"We can skip the slave boys," he said, pulling my head forward.

Our lips met, and he gave me one of those long, deep kisses that make your insides melt. It had the intensity that can only be achieved through years together. My hands slid around to the small of his back and pulled him tightly against me. I could feel how excited he was. I've often said—maybe out of a misplaced sense of self-effacement—that I think Peter is more attractive than I am, and I really do feel that way at times. But besides being a doting husband, he apparently sees something in me that gets him going. I have to confess that the first time we made love, just thinking of the fact that I aroused him gave me a buzz. And seven years later, it still does.

When our lips parted, I said, "If you do that again, I'm going to have to change my underwear."

He laughed and replied, "Let's risk it."

And we would have done that, but we were interrupted by a knock at the door, and Mother's voice saying, "Boys, are you in there?"

I grimaced. "Honest to God, she's developing the timing of a British sex farce."

Peter laughed while I went and opened the door.

"Of course we're in here," I said. "What do you think we did? Run out for a snack?"

"What on earth's the matter with you?" said Mother as she came into the room.

I could feel my face going beet red. "Oh. Nothing. I'm sorry, I'm just a little tired after the trip and all that running around."

There was a beat before she said, "Well, you'll have time to rest later." She paused and shot Peter a knowing glance that caused him to blush as well. "We have work to do now."

"Yes, Mother."

"I think the first thing we should do is go and see Larry Nelson."

"You aren't going to call him first?" I asked, clearing my throat and trying to recover myself.

"I like the element of surprise ever so much better."

"If it's ever possible to surprise him," said Peter.

Mother clucked her tongue. "I wouldn't want to give him time to make excuses for not seeing us."

"We don't even know where he is," I said, beginning to sound like the consummate whiner.

"But we do," said Mother. "At least, I think we do. Larry is with the CIA, and the CIA is at Langley." She said this with so much authority she sounded like she'd been there a hundred times.

"Langley? What's that?"

"The building that houses the CIA."

"How do you know that?"

"I asked the bellman, of course," said Mother, once again looking at me as if she thought I was terribly slow. "I'm sure everyone in this town knows what everyone else is doing. Anyway, Langley is a bit of a distance, so I think we'd better hire a car. It should be safe now. Even if those Metanayan fellows know we're in Washington, I don't think we were followed to the hotel, do you?"

I was still working on how quaint "those Metanayan fellows" sounded. She made them sound like Shriners. "No, I don't think so."

"I'll call and hire the car. You boys get cleaned up and meet me in the lobby."

"What about the dog?" I asked. I wasn't worried about him, you understand, but . . . Well, it didn't seem right to leave him in a strange hotel room.

"He's happy as a lark now that he's out of his cage. He's already curled up on the bed watching the television. He'll be fine while we're gone."

With this she breezed out of the room. Mother has a tendency to appear as if she's being propelled on the wind.

"What makes her think we need to get cleaned up?" I said to Peter.

A half hour later our rental car—a rust-red Toyota Corolla—was delivered to the door of the hotel (another one of the perks of staying somewhere classy: the car and the door-to-door delivery had been arranged by the concierge). Mother accepted the keys from the attendant and climbed behind the wheel, with me beside her and Peter in the back seat.

Mother handed me the directions the bellman had written out for her on a sheet of heavy-bond hotel stationery, and armed with a map of Washington and the surrounding areas provided by the concierge, she tried to follow the directions as I read them off. I'd like to say we reached Langley with no trouble, but Washington seems to be one big clover leaf where all the streets go around in circles without going anywhere in particular. We tried to get our bearings, driving along at a somewhat leisurely pace, and finally managed to get across the Potomac and onto the George Washington Memorial Parkway—which should have been easy since as it turned out it wasn't that far from our hotel, but it seemed to take an hour for us to accomplish it.

Once we were on the parkway, getting to our destination was more or less a breeze. The parkway is a fairly straight northwesterly shot to the CIA, with a clearly marked exit for Langley and an off ramp that practically put us in Lawrence Nelson's lap.

The building managed to be massive and nondescript at the same time, at least in comparison to historical buildings like the Capitol and the Pentagon. Mother steered the car around into the driveway to the visitor's entrance, and was stopped at the gate by a uniformed guard who emerged from a booth carrying a clipboard in his left hand. He made a sideways whirling motion with his index finger, signaling mother to roll down her window.

"State your business, please," he said peremptorily.

I leaned across her and intoned, "We're here to see Larry."

"Alex, please!" Mother said with some irritation. She turned to the guard and said politely, "We're here to see Agent Lawrence Nelson."

"Is he expecting you?"

"I really don't know," Mother replied with a shrug.

The guard raised an eyebrow, and said, "Ma'am?"

"Well, we don't have an appointment with him, if that's what you mean, but as to whether or not he's expecting us, with Larry that's difficult to tell."

"And you talk about me," I whispered to her.

"If you tell him we're here, I'm sure he'll see us."

"Names?" the guard said, raising his clipboard and poising his pen.

"Jean Reynolds, Alex Reynolds, and Peter Livesay."

"Just a moment, ma'am." The guard gave a slight nod, then went into his booth and picked up the phone.

Peter said, "Jean, you realize that you sounded like a class-A nut?"

"I was trying to speak their language."

We waited forever while the guard spoke on the phone. There's nothing like sitting in a car at the gate at the CIA while a guard checks on you to make you feel like you've done something wrong. Although Nelson knew us, and even though we worked for these people off and on, I found myself running through all my possible sins in my head. Of course, I could only come up with one that the CIA would care about, but that was what had made Nelson decide to take us on as part-timers—although two years later I was still smarting from his reference to the possibility of someone of our "ilk" coming in handy from time to time. The guard finally replaced the phone and came back to the car.

"Okay, ma'am," he said, touching two fingers to his head in a sort of salute. "Go through the gate and keep to the left. Follow the drive around to the front of the parking lot to the visitor's spots. They're clearly marked. Go in through the visitor's entrance to the desk and announce yourselves. They'll take it from there."

"You have your instructions," I said to Mother as the gate

was raised. "Follow them to the letter or you and your loved ones will suffer the consequences."

"Oh, do shut up," Mother said with a wave of her hand. She tried to sound lighthearted, but the expression on her face was pretty grave as she steered the car around the lot and into one of the visitor's spaces directly in front of the entrance. The guard hadn't been joking about them being clearly marked: Each space bore a sign that said VISITOR'S PARKING which somehow managed to look like a direct order from the president.

We climbed out of the car, and I noticed that all three of us seemed to be walking in slow motion as we approached the doors. There was something surreal about being at the actual CIA headquarters.

"If you'd told me ten years ago that I'd be visiting the CIA," I said in a mock Western accent, "I'da told you you was crazy."

"Hell, if you'd told me that *three* years ago I would've told you you were crazy," Peter replied. He didn't sound happy.

We came up to the desk, behind which were two more guards, one male and one female. The woman had jet-black hair and skin as white as a sheet. Her brows looked like they'd been carefully ruled on with a fine-point black marker. The male guard was built like a brick wall and looked about as dense. He stayed in the background.

"Yes?" said the female guard, arching her eyebrow as if she couldn't imagine us having any right to be there.

"We're here to see Agent Lawrence Nelson."

"Is he expecting you?"

"Look," said Peter, who is much quicker to lose his patience with government types than either Mother or me, "we just went through this with the guard in the parking lot. Didn't he call you?"

"Yes," said the woman without batting an eyelash.

"And?" said Peter.

The woman's right brow formed a perfect caret over her eye. "And, is Agent Nelson expecting you?"

Peter heaved an exasperated sigh. Mother said quickly, "As far as we know he is not expecting us to be here. However, if you tell him we're here, I'm sure he'll see us."

"Um-hm," said the woman, reaching for the phone on the desk. "Names?"

"Oh, Christ!" said Peter.

The woman turned her steely eyes to him and said evenly, "Is that your name, sir?"

Mother repeated our names and the guard dialed the phone. She had a brief, hushed conversation, then replaced the receiver. "Will you have a seat over there, please?" she said, pointing to a set of ultramodern chairs with curved steel legs and brown, foam-rubber seats.

"Is Larry coming down?" Mother asked.

"Someone will be down," the woman replied opaquely.

Mother shrugged and ushered us over to the chairs as if she were arranging us for a shorthanded dinner party. We were kept waiting long enough that I had time to take in the surroundings. There was a glass wall to the right that looked into the center of the building. Just past this wall was an atrium that was either lit by a skylight or by the most realistic artificial lighting I've ever seen. In the center of the atrium was a bevy of tropical plants surrounded by marble benches on which numerous people were seated, talking and eating. It was a pleasant enough scene until I got the idea in my head that perhaps this place was prepared for some sort of attack during which the occupants of the building could comfortably take refuge, like some sort of exotic bunker with a park at its center. It wouldn't have surprised me.

These thoughts were interrupted by an angry buzzer which signaled the opening of a door in the glass wall. A woman who looked young enough to have a healthy career ahead of her, and old enough to be able to hold her own in this veritable men's club, stepped through the doorway and came directly to us.

"Ms. Reynolds?" she said to Mother.

"Yes?"

"I am Agent Nelson's assistant. Will you follow me?"

"I assume you mean all three of us," said Mother with a sidelong glance at Peter and me.

"Of course."

The woman started back toward the door with the air of someone who knows her requests will be followed without question. When she reached the door it buzzed once again. I glanced at the guard's desk and the male guard was holding down a button.

We followed the woman to a bank of elevators on the right, about halfway around the atrium. She remained a few steps ahead of us and never spoke a word, which I was beginning to find unnerving. I felt like we were being led to see the school principal. When we reached the elevators she pressed the button and turned slightly so that she was almost facing us.

"Larry Nelson is here, isn't he?" said Mother in a tone that told me she was finding the silence annoying, too.

"Of course," said the woman, then fell back into silence.

We rode up to the fourth floor with her, then stepped off the elevator and followed her down a long hallway that led away from the elevators. Both sides of the hall were lined with office doors, all identical and none of them numbered. I wondered if this woman had some sort of homing signal to find the office we were looking for, or if she was silently counting her way down the hall. She came to an abrupt stop in front of one of the doors and knocked twice.

"Come," said a familiar voice from inside.

The woman opened the door and stepped aside without entering. Mother, Peter, and I filed in and the woman shut the door, closing herself on the outside.

"Well, well, well," said Agent Larry Nelson, folding his hands on a modest desk. "Look who we have here."

Nelson is one of those people who never has so much as a hair out of place, and doesn't look like it takes any effort. He has dark hair and dark skin, and is almost ostentatiously handsome, although he doesn't give any indication of knowing it. I sometimes wonder if that's part of his agent training. He didn't get up or offer any of us a handshake. He simply sat there in his usual expensive, dark blue suit, staring at us with those X-ray eyes of his. He didn't look pleased to see us.

"May we sit down?" I said.

"Of course."

He gave a single nod of his head in the direction of the two chairs in front of his desk. I pulled up a third from a table by the windows.

"You don't seem surprised to see us," I said once we were seated.

"I'm not surprised very often," he replied.

"You knew we were in town already, didn't you?" said Peter.

Nelson sat back in his high backed chair. "I knew you were in town, I didn't know you would come here. It's fairly unusual to have someone drop by."

"Next time we'll make a date," I said.

"How did you know we were in Washington?" Peter asked.

"Does it matter?"

"I guess not," Peter replied. "No explanation would make me happy."

"I know quite a few things. For example, I know that Dunn and Hamilton from the State Department are on a plane from Chicago to Washington as we speak."

"So they're the ones who told you," Peter said.

"They seem to think that now that you're out of Chicago there's no reason for them to stay there."

"We need help," said Mother. Her tone caused me to glance over at her. The expression on her face was highly displeased. She clearly was not enjoying this reception.

"That doesn't surprise me either." He was normally a blank page, but on this occasion, he was being much more terse than he would ordinarily be.

"When I talked to you the other day about the break-in," Mother continued, "I told you what was going on."

"Not quite all."

Mother contrived to look affronted but given our record it was a difficult task. Even I could see that we somehow managed to give the impression that we knew more than we did, especially

174

after my "blunder" while trying to save my life. Mother straightened her back and said, "I told you everything that we knew at the time. We've learned more since then."

"Yes," I said, taking up the thread, "like we learned what it is that everybody's looking for. A diamond."

"I think you mean *the* diamond," Nelson said wryly.

"So you've heard about it," said Mother.

Nelson sighed, having caught Mother's tone. He leaned forward, resting his arms on his desk. "When I spoke with Agent Hamilton—at your insistence, I might add—he explained to me that somehow you have managed to get yourselves mixed up in what may well become an international incident."

"It wasn't our fault!" I was coming dangerously close to whining.

"I have no doubt of that. It never is."

I thought it would be better to get back on track than to try to argue that point. Given our activities of the last three years, I would've lost. "What we told you was true. We didn't know what those people were looking for when we called you, and we don't have it. That's the problem. These Metanayan people are out to kill us because they think we have it and won't give it back to them."

"Just yesterday Alex and Peter were attacked by them. If I hadn't come home with Frank O'Neil, I don't like to think what might've happened."

"So we need your help," I said.

"And what help would that be?"

"The Metanayans are here—somewhere in the Washington area. Can't you locate them and tell them that we don't have their damn diamond and get them off our backs?"

Nelson sat back in his chair. "You know that I can't get involved in any case being carried out on our native soil."

"What?" Mother exclaimed, followed closely by Peter and me. "What are you on about? Every bloody time we've seen you you've been carrying out some shenanigans 'ere on native soil."

"Only under very special circumstances," Nelson said with a

slight tilt of his head, "and that at a very limited level. I can't get involved in this. I can't interfere in something being handled by the State Department. It would mean my job."

"It may mean our *lives*," said Peter. "I would think that constituted special circumstances."

Nelson looked at him for a full minute before responding. "I'm curious: Why didn't you just go to Dunn and Hamilton and ask them to deliver this message for you?"

Once again, he looked like he already knew the answer. "Because we don't trust them and they don't trust us," I said quickly. Nelson looked at me and raised an eyebrow, so I continued. "We don't know that it was these Metanayans who broke into our house the first time. It may very well have been your people—" He started to correct me, so I did it myself. ". . . Sorry, it may very well have been the State Department people trying to get the thing back."

"And aside from that," said Peter, "we think that Dunn and Hamilton are more interested in getting the diamond back than they are in the fact that these people have killed two of our friends. We happen to believe that human life is more valuable than some stinking stone, no matter how valuable it is or how many people pray to it!"

"And why don't they trust *you*?" Nelson asked without emotion.

"They don't think we're telling them the truth," I said. "They seem to think we have the diamond."

"Are you sure you don't?"

Mother's brow furrowed so deeply I thought she might crease her skull. "Larry, exactly how daft do you think we are?"

"I'll reserve judgment on that."

She ignored him. "If we had that diamond and had hoped to sell the blasted thing, we certainly would've given that up as a bad job and returned it after all that's happened."

"Not that that would save our lives at this point," I added. "Apparently the Metanayans are a vengeful people."

"What we have to do is get them to understand that we don't

have it—that we never had it," said Peter.

"And I would think hearing it from you would carry some weight," said Mother.

Nelson looked at her for a few moments with his usual impassive face. Mother was the only person I knew of who could occasionally break through the wall into the little human being that lived somewhere inside this man.

"Jean, you have to understand first of all that as a representative of the CIA I cannot approach these people about this. Secondly, from what I understand the Metanayans are a very important factor to the Thai government, and right at the moment our two governments are in the midst of negotiating—"

"Don't say it!" Peter exclaimed hotly. "You're not going to tell us that you can't hunt down these killers because of some stupid trade agreement you're all banking on."

Nelson looked at him and said nothing for a few seconds. Apparently Peter had hit the nail on the head. "All I can say is that the talks are at a critical stage, and even if they weren't, any indication on our side that we were somehow working against their government would cause serious problems, both in the present negotiations and in the agreements that already exist."

"Money," I said, with enough contempt that I sounded exactly like my husband. "You're willing to do anything you can to placate them, even at the cost of the lives of two people who were worth more than the lot of you put together."

"Not *anything*," Nelson replied coolly.

"Nelson, these people have killed two of our friends!" I said.

"And do you have proof of that?"

"What?"

"Do you have proof that they're the murderers?"

"Yes! The one who was going to cut me open admitted to it!"

"Was there anyone else there?"

I knew he was playing devil's advocate, and it was really making me angry. "Did there have to be?"

"Yes. A witness. If your police in Chicago had any evidence then the people who killed your friends would already be in jail.

On your word alone no jury in the world would convict them."

"But the police can't even find them, and—"

"Alex," said Mother firmly. I stopped in the middle of my argument and looked at her. "First things first. Let's try to save our own necks, then we can see if we can put the noose around the others." She turned to Nelson and said, "Are we to understand that we're to receive no help from you whatsoever?"

"No," said Nelson as calmly as ever, "I didn't mean that we were just going to leave you swinging in the wind."

"Oh, there's comforting news," said Mother.

"I can go through proper channels and see if we can't persuade the parties involved that you don't have the diamond."

"Meaning Dunn and Hamilton?" I asked.

"Meaning everyone involved. It's possible that if Dunn and Hamilton didn't believe you were telling the truth, they may have conveyed that, knowingly or unknowingly, to the Metanayans. Perhaps we can correct that."

For the first time I was beginning to feel that there might be a light at the end of the tunnel and a chance that we wouldn't all end up kabobbed. I was wrenched from this momentary respite when Mother said, "Alex?"

"What?"

She gave me her sternest motherly look. "Tell him."

"Tell him what?"

She raised her eyebrows and cocked her head toward Nelson, signaling me to go ahead. Then it hit me.

"Oh." I turned to Nelson rather sheepishly and said, "It might not be . . . exactly . . . that easy to get the Metanayans to believe that we don't have the diamond."

"Why?" Nelson said after a beat.

"Well, when they attacked me, I told them I didn't have it . . . but then I sort of told them that I did have it."

There was another slight pause before Nelson said, "Why did you do that?"

"It was the only way I could think of to get away from them."

Nelson sighed. "Well, we'll see if we can correct that."

"Through proper channels?" said Peter with a little snort.

"Um-hm."

"There's a bit of hurry-up involved here," said Mother, "since we're going to be next in our graves if these people aren't convinced in time. So while you're going through proper channels, I think we need to take matters into our own hands."

"What do you mean?" Nelson said.

"I think we should go straight to the source."

"What?"

"There must be someone in charge of the Metanayan Temple and their people here. I think we should go to him straightaway and see if we can't reason with him. They can't all be crazy."

"I wouldn't count on that," I said.

Nelson folded his hands on his desk. "I don't think that's advisable."

"Of course *you* don't. It isn't you with your neck on the chopping block. Now can you tell us where their temple is?" When Nelson didn't respond right away, Mother added, "I have to believe you know where they are."

Nelson continued to look at Mother. I assume he was debating with himself whether or not to give us the information.

"Really, Larry," Mother continued, "if you don't tell us we'll just have to start asking around until we find someone who will. And if we do that the Metanayans are liable to find out what we're doing and find us before we find them. If that 'appens, we've 'ad it."

Nelson knew her well enough to know that she wasn't making an idle threat. He was completely still for a moment, then he reached down behind his desk, pulled out a drawer, and retrieved a single sheet of paper. He closed the drawer, straightened up, and handed the sheet to Mother.

"Of course, we keep files on all types of groups that are operating in the United States but are based outside American soil. We do have a file on the Metanayans, and I pulled it the moment I first heard they were involved. Until now they haven't caused anyone any trouble. Of course, nobody has caused any trouble for them, either, so we had no idea how they would respond in adverse circumstances. That is the address of the Metanayan temple."

Mother stood and took the paper from him. "Thank you," she said curtly. "Come along, boys."

She headed for the door and Peter and I got up and trailed along after her just like Jane and Michael Banks.

"Jean," Nelson said, right as she put her hand on the doorknob. The three of us stopped and turned around. "These people are very, very dangerous, as you well know by now. I hope that once you've given it some thought, you'll reconsider this crazy idea of yours and let the professionals handle it."

"The professionals," Mother said down her nose, "have made a proper muck-up of it already, thank you!"

Not one to waste a dramatic exit line, she flipped the door open and marched out. It would have been quite effective except that the door banged into my toe and I let out a very unlovely cry of pain before limping over the threshold supported by my husband.

I don't usually tussle with my mother, mainly because both of us believe in leading as harmonious an existence as possible, and because she's usually right. But this wasn't a usual situation.

"You're not going with us!" I said loudly, for the third time.

"You're bloody well not going there alone!"

"I won't be alone." I could feel Peter rolling his eyes in the back seat.

"I'm going with you!" Mother repeated, slapping her hand on the steering wheel as she maneuvered the car back onto the George Washington Memorial Parkway. "It's far too dangerous for the two of you to be on your own."

"Mother, it's Wednesday night. I hope the head of the temple will be there so we can talk to him, but there probably won't be anyone there at all. Who would be in a temple on Wednesday night—"

"Honestly," she interrupted, "I obviously failed in your religious upbringing as well."

"...so what possible danger could there be?" I concluded with only a slight pause between the halves of my sentence.

"There it is," she retorted. "If there won't be any danger, then there's no reason I shouldn't come with you!"

"The hell there isn't," I said hotly. "I said there *probably* won't be any danger, but there *might* be!" I realized, though not soon enough, that I was trying unsuccessfully to debate both sides of my own lame argument. I hoped she wouldn't notice that I'd just said it would and wouldn't be dangerous at the same time, but trying to get anything by her is like trying to build a house on a mud slide.

"All the more reason I should be there. If it's dangerous you could use my help. It wouldn't be the first time I pulled your chestnuts out of the fire, now would it?" She said it nicely but it was accompanied by a smile sly enough to make me feel like a baboon.

"Yes," I said weakly, "but that doesn't mean I would purposely lead you into danger."

"It doesn't?" Mother and Peter said in unison. I shot a harsh look over my shoulder to let my husband know that I expected him to back me up even when I wasn't making any sense.

"I don't care!" I exclaimed. "It doesn't matter what argument you try to come up with, you are not going with us and that's that!"

And that, of course, is always the wrong tack to take with my mother. There was a momentary, stony silence, and enough tension in the air to make my eardrums vibrate. After a pregnant pause, Mother smiled and said, "Fine."

"Look, I didn't mean—"

"No, no," she said broadly, "that's quite all right. Really. It's fine. You're only looking out for my safety, and I appreciate that."

I stared at the side of her face, searching it for any sign of sarcasm. I didn't find any.

"On second thought, I think it would be safer to have you with us."

THIRTEEN

Mother was quiet all the way to the temple, which scared me because it's a sign that her wheels and gears are working overtime. The address that Nelson had given us was a few miles east and north of the hotel on Fifteenth Street. There were a lot of cars on the street—fewer taxis than we'd yet encountered anywhere in our short stay in Washington—and almost no foot traffic at all. The street included some apartment buildings and a few smaller shops, but nothing that even remotely resembled a church of any creed or nationality. We were expecting something like the Buddhist temple that we'd visited back in Chicago, but when we located the address it turned out to be a rather unimpressive storefront. Dusk was passing on to darkness as we pulled into a parking space about a block away from the building.

"That can't be it, can it?" I said as we walked back to the place.

"It's the address Nelson gave us. You suppose maybe he just gave us a dummy address to keep us running around in circles while he goes through those channels of his?"

"It wouldn't surprise me."

"Funny," Peter said after a long silence. "Every time he said he'd go through proper channels I pictured him slithering through a sewer."

I laughed a little too loudly at this, which showed that I was much more nervous than I was trying to let on.

"What do we do when we get there?" said Peter, laying a hand for a moment on the small of my back. Apparently my anxiety hadn't escaped him.

"Play it by ear."

"You're talking as if I'm not coming in with you," said Mother.

I'd been dreading this moment. I'd let her come this far—if anyone could ever be said to be "letting" my mother do anything—but I really hoped I could keep her from going in with us. On the way I'd thought of something that might make her happy. "I was hoping you would stand lookout for us."

"Lookout?" she said, raising her eyebrows as her voice slid up an octave.

"Of course. We need someone as lookout. If the three of us go in there and something goes wrong, we'll be cooked. Nobody else know we're here."

"Nelson knows," Peter said unhelpfully.

"He doesn't know we're here *now*," I replied, shooting him a warning glance. I turned to Mother. "I want you to stand lookout. If there's any sign that something's gone wrong, or if you think we've been in there too long, call Nelson or the police or anybody, but get help!"

Mother gave me a slow, appraising look, then she said, "Right. I'll be over there."

Before I could reply, she skittled across the street and secreted herself in a darkened doorway.

Peter and I continued to the store and, after taking a deep breath, went in, even though there was nothing on the outside of the store to indicate that there was any kind of temple inside. A bell over the door clanged loudly as the door opened and closed, but nobody appeared in answer to it. The interior was choked with oriental doodads that looked a little too realistic to appeal to the general tourist trade. There were musty-looking oriental rugs, small gold (or gilt) statues of different Asian figures, large, ornately carved wooden chests, and smaller cabinets that looked like they did dual service as staircases. There was also a large array of Buddhas: small, large, and in between, made of varieties of materials. Some of the small ones had in their laps glass cups that held votive candles; they looked like some strange hybrid of Buddhism and Catholicism. The air was thick with a heavy, unrecognizable aroma that wafted from one of the brass incense burners displayed on a glass counter near the back of the store. The incense combined with the stale air and the closeness caused by the congested wares were all working together to make it difficult to breathe.

"Is anybody here?" I called out softly. It wasn't the kind of place where you felt comfortable raising your voice.

There was no answer except for the silence that seemed to buzz in our ears. Peter and I looked at each other. He looked like he didn't know what we should do next, either. I was about to say that he was probably right about Nelson when suddenly he raised his index finger and said quietly, "Shh. Listen."

I strained my ears to try to pick up what he was hearing, but at first didn't get it.

"Do you hear that?" he said, still keeping his voice low. "It sounds like chanting or something."

I listened even more intently, and after a few seconds I realized what he was talking about. There was a very low sound that seemed to be coming from somewhere in the distance. It probably had been going on since we entered, but since it wasn't exactly singing and it seemed to be pretty far away, neither of us noticed it at first.

"Where is it coming from?" I said.

Peter cocked his head for a moment, then went over to a curtained doorway behind the glass counter. He parted the curtains slightly and listened.

"Back here somewhere."

He glanced back at me and I shrugged, then followed him through the curtains.

The back room was even more choked with goods than the front, but they were packed neatly in boxes which were stamped MADE IN THAILAND. We made our way down the narrow aisle formed by the crates, and the humming noise seemed to get a little louder as we neared the back of the building.

"I don't like this," I said, sounding just like the ineffectual heroine in some B-grade jungle movie from the thirties. But it was very dark and the noise was beginning to spook me.

As we neared the back of the storeroom, we saw what looked at first to be a railing sitting in the middle of nowhere and not attached to anything. But when we reached it, it turned out to be the top railing of a staircase that spiraled down through the floor to a rather dank-looking basement, although actually seeing anything down there was next to impossible.

"You first," said Peter with a smile.

"I really don't like this," I replied. "But if that temple's down there, we might as well go ahead and see if we can find the head of it. We've come this far."

I heaved a sigh that seemed to vibrate out of me in sporadic bursts, then began the climb down the stairs as quietly as I could. Peter followed behind me. Once we were below the first floor level the chanting seemed louder but still curiously distant.

Halfway down the stairs I turned back to Peter and whispered, "You don't think they could keep a giant gorilla down here, do you?"

"Don't make me laugh!" he said, putting a hand over his mouth.

"Just trying to lighten the moment." I continued downward, with a renewed admiration of Fay Wray's pluck.

We reached the bottom of the stairs and found ourselves in a wide vestibule that had been partitioned off from the rest of the basement by a set of dark, velvet-looking curtains that hung from ceiling to floor. Apparently they were the reason the chanting seemed muffled. The curtains were thick enough to absorb almost anything—*even a scream,* my mind insisted on adding. The little anteroom we were in was lit only by tall candles in sconces on the walls. The floor and walls were dank-smelling cement. It reminded me of every movie I'd ever seen about a cult. Along the wall behind the stairs was a long set of wooden pegs. Many of the pegs were empty, but the rest held long black robes that hung by their hoods on their individual pegs.

We exchanged glances, and I whispered, "The better part of valor? It might give us a chance to get the lay of the land before we take any unnecessary chances."

"Unnecessary chances," Peter managed to snort softly. We donned robes and flipped the hoods up over our heads, hoping that if we kept our faces to the floor we wouldn't be recognized until we had time to identify who the head of the place was, and decide on some way to get to talk to him alone.

Once we were properly clad, we went to the break in the center of the curtains, slid it aside and stopped cold before we stepped in. I had expected a bunch of people squatting on the cold basement floor in a more-or-less bare room. What we found instead was a room that challenged the Llasa Buddhist Temple in style and elegance. Everywhere there was red and gold, and a long altar stretched across the back wall.

Dozens of people, all identical in their black robes, sat cross-legged on mats on the floor staring at the altar and chanting. Now that we were in the room I could tell it wasn't just a hum; they were actually saying words, but they kept their voices so low and static that it sounded like one tone. There was nobody at the altar, so we had no way of knowing whether or not anyone was leading them.

We stepped through the curtain's opening. There was one man standing to the side, apparently some sort of sentry. He nodded once and we nodded back, trying to make it look as much like his movement as possible. As we continued into the room, the man stepped out through the opening and closed the curtains behind him.

The air was even heavier there than it had been in the shop up above. All of these people so close together, the lack of windows, and the chanting all seemed to suck what little air there was right out of the room. Peter touched my arm and cocked his head slightly in the direction of an open space on a mat to our right. I followed him and we sat. I'm about two years in a health club away from attempting the lotus position, so I tried to keep my legs hidden under the robe so that nobody would notice that I was just sitting.

I scanned the room backward and forward, looking for whoever might be their leader, hoping maybe he would have—I don't know, a crown, or a hat, or maybe the high priest of this religion got to wear a red robe instead of a black one or something—but my original assessment had been correct: All of them were identical, and from the back there was no way of telling any of them apart. The "congregation" could have been made up of every race and nationality for all I knew.

The heat, the stagnant air, and the chanting were beginning to lull me into a semi-comatose state, when I happened to look at the altar, and saw something I hadn't noticed before. At first I thought I was hallucinating from the lack of oxygen, but as the light dawned on me, I almost screamed "Oh my God!", but caught myself in time to make it sound like a verbal stomach cramp.

Peter was looking at me with a mixture of concern and admonition on his face, but I couldn't bother about my slip at that moment. I nodded toward the altar as frantically as I could and still keep a low profile, trying to get him to look at it. He finally turned his eyes to it, and after a few seconds turned back to me, his face one big question mark.

As little as we wanted to draw attention to ourselves, there was something I had to know. I turned to the black-robed man sitting on my other side.

"Excuse me . . ." I said in an anxious whisper. I didn't know exactly how one begins when one is interrupting someone's chanting. He turned a surprised eye at me. ". . . Please, excuse me . . . but that thing on the altar—is that the Metanayan Buddha?"

"It is a replica," he said in a soft voice that sounded scandalized at the idea of anyone talking in the temple.

I looked to the Buddha and back to the man. "A *scale* model?"

"No, no, it is an exact replica." He held me in his gaze for a moment as if wondering if I was going to interrupt him any further, then turned away and resumed his chant.

I leaned over to Peter and whispered excitedly, "We've got to get out of here!"

"What is it?"

"Never mind! Come on!"

We both got up and headed for the break in the curtains. Peter pulled them aside and we both stepped through. The curtains were immediately closed behind us, and both of us were set upon by attackers whom we could only vaguely see in the dark candlelight of the temple's anteroom. There seemed to be three of them, but since we were all clad in those ridiculous flowing robes, all I could really see during the altercation was black cloth flailing in the air. The man assigned to me threw his left arm tightly around my chest and slapped his right hand over my mouth. I could feel a tightness in my neck, and the threat that was clearly implied: One wrong word or move and he could simply twist my head and snap my neck. Once we were subdued, the third man crossed in front of us into view. I recognized him immediately.

"I told you that if you didn't return the diamond to us, the consequences for you would be dire. We tried to do it the right way."

Since a response seemed to be called for, the hand on my mouth loosened. "You didn't tell me you were one of 'us,' " I said.

"Who is he?" Peter struggled to say.

The hand had not retightened across my mouth, so I had enough mobility to turn my head and look at my husband. He was being held much the same as I was. We looked like participants in a really ugly hazing party. "This is the nice man who popped out from behind our garage and warned me about keeping the diamond." I turned back to the guy and said, "I just can't see how you could work in the Thai import company in Chicago and be the head of this crazy religion here." As if to prove my point, the man holding me tightened his grip painfully when I said the word *crazy*.

"I'm not a Metanayan priest," said the man with a very unpleasant smile. "I'm just one of the— I believe you would call it the flock?"

"I wouldn't dare call it anything," I replied. "Look, we came here to see your . . . to see the head of this place."

"You must be mad."

"No, I'm not. We don't have your goddamn diamond, and I was hoping whoever was in charge would have enough of his brains left that we could get him to understand that!"

The man didn't reply. He looked as if he didn't know whether to think we were the dumbest pair of queers on the face of the earth, or to admire our bravery for doing something so . . . well, dumb.

He looked over my shoulder at the man holding me and said, "Bring them along." Then he headed into a dark corner at the end of the row of wooden pegs, to a door that I hadn't noticed before. We weren't so much dragged as we were pushed awkwardly along after him. The hand had reclamped tightly over my mouth so I couldn't utter a sound of protest. The third man gave a single knock on the door and then went in. We were pushed in after him.

Once inside, the door was slammed behind us and our captors released their hold and stepped back, remaining an obvious presence so that we'd know there was no use in trying to escape.

The room was small but elegant in the same style as the temple outside. The walls were deep red and so was the carpet. On the wall to the right there was a painting of a smiling Buddha with a glittering jewel in his navel. With what I now thought I knew, I almost cringed when I saw the picture.

A very small bespectacled man sat in a red velvet chair behind an oak table. He had a thick graying mustache and amused brown eyes. He was smoking a pipe with an inordinantly long, curved stem, and a thick stream of smoke rose from the business end. He was clad in a red silk robe. At least I'd been right about one thing: He did dress differently from the rest of them. But at that moment I didn't think the words "I was right" would be a comforting epitaph.

"So, you wanted to meet the High Priest of the Metanayan Temple," said the garage man. "Here he is." He gave a deferential bow in the direction of the priest and backed away.

"Yes?" said the priest. "You must be Alex Reynolds, the man who is holding the stone of our Buddha hostage."

"No, I'm not!" I said, sounding exactly like a twelve year old. "I mean, I am Alex Reynolds, but I'm not holding anything hostage."

"It's rather the other way around, don't you think?" said Peter.

"Really?" said the priest with a wicked smile. "Our people have followed the stone from the temple in Thailand, to the doll company, to Washington and then to Chicago. The trail ends with you."

"No," I said, feeling bold with anger now that I was face to face with this guy, "the trail ended with our friends Mason and Ryan. Two of the sweetest guys on the face of this earth who were murdered for nothing by your people!"

"They were sacrificed because they had something that belonged to us—the significance of which you could never understand—and they refused to return it. And now it has passed on to you." His face reddened and his eyes hardened. "But I tell you that the trail *will* end with you!" He slammed his fist on the table so suddenly that I'm ashamed to say I was startled and jumped back slightly.

He shouted something in his language, waving a hand in our direction. Apparently he was giving an order to his two thugs, because Peter and I were both grabbed from behind and before we knew what was happening we were each pinned to the wall. I recognized the two men who had been holding us at once: They were the same two men who had attacked us in our house. Both of them had produced those horrible ceremonial knives that I had seen before and were holding them to our necks as if we were a pair of prize turkeys that were about to become Thanksgiving dinner.

"My, my," I said through my constricted throat. "Everyone has come to Washington. Popular place."

The priest rose from behind his table and crossed to us. He brought his face up to within a couple of inches of mine, and said, "I think it doesn't matter now whether you tell us where the diamond is or not. You have defiled the diamond with your tricks and your stubbornness, and you will pay the price." He stopped suddenly and raised his eyebrows, a little smile appearing on his face, as if he'd just had a new idea. "But perhaps . . . perhaps you may still save your mother. Perhaps if you tell us where the diamond is now, we will let her live . . . but only perhaps. As for saving yourselves, I'm afraid we're past that point."

I was about to be gutted like some decrepit old building, only more painfully, and all I could think of was the scene in *Raiders of the Lost Ark* where the leering Nazi is threatening Marion with a red-hot poker. Marion says she could be reasonable, and the Nazi sneered back, "That time is past." *Oh Christ!* I thought, *I'm going to die with cheesy movie dialogue on my lips!*

"Where is the diamond?" the priest demanded loudly, the two assailants shoving us hard into the wall again for punctuation.

I've never really thought of myself as valorous, but at that moment, knowing that my life was about to end, all I could think of was that I had an opportunity, however slight, to make a last grand gesture and hopefully save my mother. And it wasn't going to be an empty gesture, because now that I'd seen the statue on their alter, I really did think I knew where the diamond was.

"I . . . I . . . ." I stammered, knowing that once I'd complete the sentence it would all be over.

But before I could say another word, there was a high-pitched, blood-curdling scream from the little anteroom outside.

"FIRE! FIRE!" the voice screamed.

There was only a split second before all hell broke loose. The door was flung open from the outside by one of the black-robed Metanayans, and we could easily see that there really was a fire blazing precariously close to the curtains separating the anteroom from the temple. In fact, for a moment I thought it actually was the curtains that were ablaze. Our two assailants were startled enough that they released us, and even the priest seemed too surprised by the scene outside to be concerned about our whereabouts. We darted out the door only a moment before they realized what we were doing and took off after us.

The Metanayan who'd opened the door was racing toward the spiral staircase, and we followed, caught in the surge of people as the "congregation" made a chaotic dash toward the staircase, the only way out of this firetrap of a building. The crowd swept us out of the grasp of our pursuers, who had lost their advantage in the brief moment it had taken them to realized we were fleeing. As we ran I kept thinking, *Torn Curtain, Torn Curtain, Torn Curtain. Don't get separated from Peter or you'll never see him again.*

The Metanayan we were following reached the bottom of the stairs with Peter and me close behind. We clambered up the stairs, all the while being shoved from behind by the others who were desperately trying to save themselves. As we reached the top of the stairs, the overhead sprinkler system finally kicked on, drenching the screaming mob and managing to whip them into an ever higher state of hysteria.

We ran through the narrow lane of boxes in the back room, through the shop, and out onto the street. When we reached the curb, the Metanayan who'd been leading us suddenly wheeled around and yelled, "Get to the car!"

"What?!" I shouted. I stopped in my tracks, completely dumbfounded, and Peter came to an equally abrupt stop beside me. The wet, hooded Metanayans continued to spill out into the street.

"Get to the car!"

"Mother!" I said loudly, finally recognizing the voice from beneath the hood.

"Oh, *do* shut up and run, won't you? They're right behind us!"

"No wonder I was thinking of *Torn Curtain!*" I said crossly. "We've been rescued by Julie Andrews!"

"Hoods up, dears," she said as she took off down the street.

We put our hoods up and took off after her. She was right, of course. People were swarming out of the temple and taking off in all directions. With our hoods up, from behind our pursuers wouldn't be able to tell us from anyone else.

"Give me the keys," said Mother as we reached the car. I tossed them to her without question because she always was a better getaway driver than I could ever be. When it comes to some things, Mother has absolutely no nerve. And as she'd just demonstrated, when it comes to others she has all the nerve in the world, only of a different kind.

"What in the hell were you doing in there?" I demanded once we were speeding down the street.

"Saving your skins, it would seem." Once again she had that exhilarated look on her face that worries me so much.

"Christ!" said Peter as he struggled his way out of his robe. "Who was it that said a boy's best friend is his mother?"

"Norman Bates," I snapped back at him. Then I turned to Mother and said, "You were supposed to *go* for help!"

"Go for it? By the time I'd gotten anyone here, you would've been dead."

"I suppose," I said grudgingly. "Did you at least *wait* before following us in?"

"A little," she said. "I looked in the window for a while and didn't see anybody, so I went in. I suppose I followed the same route you did, but when I found the staircase, I didn't go down it right away."

"You surprise me," I said wryly.

"Well, I *have* read *Alice in Wonderland* once or twice. Something that you'd do well to do. Anyway, I watched and listened at the top of the staircase, so I saw when they caught you and dragged you into that room. The rest you know."

"No, the rest we don't know," I said.

She looked confused for a second, then said, "Oh. Right. Well, when they took you I climbed down the stairs and got into this getup." She gave a little tug at her robe. "And was trying to think of what to do when I hit on it. They always say that when you yell 'fire' you have a better chance of getting help than if you just yell 'help.'"

"But you set the place on fire!" I said incredulously.

"I didn't set the *place* on fire, darling. Do you think I'm mad?"

She didn't pause long enough for me to answer.

"It wouldn't have done to just stand there yelling 'fire' like the village idiot. Anyone with working eyes in their heads would've been able to see that there was no fire. So I had to risk it. I made a pile of some of those robes and set them off with one of those candles on the wall. I mean, I'm not completely balmy—I did check first to make sure they had sprinklers on the ceiling. And the whole place was cement."

"Except for the curtains," I added ungraciously. "Is that what you call getting our chestnuts out of the fire? By setting us on fire yourself? You could've killed us all!"

"Well, darling, you were dead anyway," she said with a nonchalant shrug.

"Have you completely lost your mind?"

She looked at me pointedly and said, "When it comes to protecting you, yes. Do you have any doubts they would've killed you? I would've set the whole damn town ablaze to get you out of there."

I didn't know what to say. 'Thank you' seemed so inappropriate at that moment.

"Our most immediate concern, though," Mother continued, "is what in the bloody hell are we going to do now?"

"We've got to get back!" I replied excitedly. "I know where the diamond is!"

"What?" Peter and Mother exclaimed in unison.

"I know where it is! We've had it all the time!"

"Then we have to get back to Chicago tonight," said Peter from the back seat.

I turned around and looked at him. "No, we don't. We brought it with us!"

"I didn't realize it until I saw that goddamn Buddha!" I said as Mother unlocked the door to her hotel suite. "All this time, all these people have been talking about the stone coming from Buddha's navel, and like a pack of idiots, we just assumed that it was huge. But they had a replica of the Metanayan Buddha at that temple, and it's less than a foot tall!"

Mother opened the door and switched on the lights as she walked in. We followed her, and Peter closed the door behind us. The dog was lying on the bed with his forepaws crossed in front of him as if he were praying. And well he should have been. I could have killed him, if only for the fact that he couldn't talk. If he could, it would have saved us a lot of trouble all the way around. He lifted his head and looked at us curiously as we approached the bed.

"It's okay, doggie," said Mother. "Nobody's going to hurt you."

She reached down and turned that ridiculous Zsa Zsa Gabor collar of his around until she found the clasp, then undid it and slipped it off. The three of us stood there peering at the glittering rhinestones, trying to figure out which one was the stone that had cost so many people their lives. At first they all looked the same to me.

"I thought Hamilton said the diamond was purple," I said.

"No, not purple, violet," Peter said.

"With all the blood that's been spilled over it, it should be red," I replied.

Mother continued to turn the collar around between her fingers, till suddenly she stopped and pointed to one stone with the nail of her thumb. "There it is."

"Where?"

"There." She slipped her nail under the stone and pried it off, letting it roll down into her palm.

"But that's not violet," I said.

"Look closely at it."

Peter and I stared down into her palm as if she was holding the secret of life. The stone caught the light and glittered in her hand, and at first I thought my eyes might be playing tricks on me, but I actually thought I caught a hint of violet.

"He didn't say the stone was violet," Mother explained, "he said it had a natural violet cast. Very, very light violet."

"But this stone is so small," Peter said. "It can't be worth all that much money."

Mother pursed her lips. "Well, it could be worth as much as seventy or eighty thousand." Both Peter and I turned slowly toward her, wondering at her sudden demonstration of gem valuation. She blinked. "It's not as if I've never been to a jewelry store before."

"But this thing . . . this thing isn't even worth that much money . . . and all these people have been killed over it!"

"Intrinsic value," Peter said, reminding me of Hamilton's words. "It wasn't the money."

"Oh, good Lord!" Mother exclaimed as she sank down onto the bed. She held the stone between her thumb and index finger. "I can't believe we've been so stupid! Do you realize what this means? This is why Ryan didn't want to take the doggie with him when he went home the night after he stayed with us."

"But why did he go home at all?" Peter asked.

"Because he didn't want us to know he was making plans to get out of town," I said. "What I don't know is why he was leaving—because he was afraid for his life after Mason was killed, or because he wanted to get away with the diamond?"

"Well, we'll never know the answer to that one, I'm afraid," said Mother.

I looked at the diamond, then down at the dog, and I couldn't help laughing.

"What?" said Peter.

I shook my head. "It's just so like Mason to put a precious stone like that on that damn dog's collar."

Peter nodded. "He probably never wanted to sell it at all. He just wanted to know what it was worth. He probably always intended to leave it on that collar."

The three of us fell into a contemplative silence that was finally interrupted when Mother said, "So, the question is, what are we going to do with it now that we've found it?"

I looked at my mother, the gleam in her eye reminding me of all the little peccadillos she and I have gotten into and out of, with the help of my husband, over the past couple of years. Out of the corner of my eye, I noticed Peter looking back and forth between Mother and me. He looked concerned. And he should have been.

"Mother," I said, "I think it's time for your Lucy Ricardo routine. . . ."

FOURTEEN

We talked well into the night, and I have to admit that when all was said and done, Mother had led us in coming up with a plan that didn't seem quite so much like one of our usual exercises in lunacy. It was a plan that, if it worked out, might manage to bring the two murderers to justice, and bring a satisfactory resolution to the rest of it.

The following morning, after enjoying room service in Mother's suite, I was relegated the job of calling Nelson.

"Yes?" He gave his usual, terse greeting.

"It's Alex Reynolds."

"Yes?"

"I have something to tell you."

He sighed and said, "Yes?"

"I have the diamond."

There was a slight pause before he said, "I thought you said you didn't have it."

"Well . . . I do. I didn't when we talked, but I found it."

"You found it," he repeated slowly. "You didn't have it, but you found it . . . in Washington."

"That's right."

There was a beat, then he said, "Well, fine. Then you should turn it over."

"Not so fast," I said. I took a deep breath, because this was going to be the difficult part. "We're willing to turn over the diamond, but not unless we can be assured that the men who killed Mason and Ryan will be caught."

There was a longer pause this time. Through the phone I could fairly hear the wheels and gears spinning in Nelson's head. "Why do I have a feeling you're about to make me very unhappy?"

"Come on, Larry," I said, using his first name to irritate him. "I know you well enough to know that you're just as interested in justice as we are."

"All right," he replied. He still sounded suspicious.

I glanced at Mother for encouragement, then said, "Well, so, we're willing to turn over the diamond, but only to the murderers."

"What?" I'd actually caught him by surprise.

"That's right. I know there's no evidence against them, so what I want to do is try to get a confession out of them. And for that we're going to need your help."

There was a beat before Nelson replied. "I would be neglecting my duty if I failed to say at this point that I think you've lost your mind."

"You have the means to bug me . . . or wire me, or whatever you guys call it. You can listen in when I turn the diamond over to them, and maybe I can get them to tell me what they told me before—that they killed our friends."

"And exactly how do you intend to get them to confess? By asking them politely if they killed your friends?"

"By refusing to hand the diamond over until I know. Why should they balk at saying it again? They already said it once."

He sighed like a parent who is getting frustrated with trying to reason with a child. "Assuming I was willing to be involved in such a thing—and I'm not admitting for a moment that I am—you'd be taking a ridiculous amount of risk. They're likely to kill you then and there."

"They're not stupid," I said, "They'll know that you guys are around somewhere."

"Alex . . ."

"Look, according to their priest, they're going to kill us anyway. So if they don't do it right away, there's a chance that you'll be able to get them for the murders. If we can't get them this way, then our days are numbered anyway. I'd rather go trying to catch them then just sitting at home and waiting for it to happen."

There was a lengthy silence after this, during which I crossed my fingers and hoped that Nelson would actually buy what I was trying to sell him. Peter was sitting in a chair at the desk in Mother's room, Mother sat on the edge of the bed, and both of them were staring at me intently, waiting as anxiously as I was for the answer.

"Unless the Metanayans are fools," Nelson said at last, "—and you say they're not stupid—they'll know the reason you want to bring these two men out into the open. They'll never fall for it."

"They're zealots," I said, using the term that Hamilton had used to explain the behavior of this strange cult. "They may realize what I'm trying to do, but they want the diamond back. They may want it back enough to sacrifice two of their people."

There was another long pause, then Nelson said, "What do you hope to get out of this, Alex?"

"What do you mean?"

"Just what I said."

I thought for a few seconds, then said, "Justice. The same thing we've always wanted; for the guys that killed Mason and Ryan to get what's coming to them."

"And the diamond?"

"I don't care about the diamond," I replied, hoping that I hadn't said it too quickly. Nelson often makes me feel transparent. It's as if he's spent so much time figuring out schemes that he's thought of the outcome before you even try it.

"You would just turn the diamond over after we've apprehended these guys."

"Of course I would! I don't want to hold on to the damn thing!"

There was a beat before he said, "If I consider doing this, I'll still have to go through proper channels."

"By all means," I said agreeably. "I think Dunn and Hamilton should be in on it. I mean, eventually the diamond would have to be turned over to them anyway, right?"

"Right." I could swear the tone in Nelson's voice carried a hint of amusement. "Let me get back to you."

With that we both hung up.

"Well?" said Peter.

"I don't know." I was still staring at the phone as if maybe I could get the answer from it. "He sounded . . . funny. I don't know, he said he's going to go through proper channels."

"If I know Larry Nelson," said Mother, "he'll make it happen. He'll want these people caught as much as we do. But what did he say about the diamond?"

"Nothing."

Mother shook her head slowly. "I don't like it. Why would he believe so readily that we'd turn the diamond over to these people when everything's over?"

Peter said, "Because he knows we've thought it out as well as he has. He knows that if the diamond becomes evidence in a murder case, it will be impounded here and the Thai government won't get it back for years, if they ever do."

"But Nelson's sharp," I said. "If he thinks we're up to something, he'll try to counter it."

"Not at the cost of losing the murderers," Mother said with more confidence than I felt.

For some reason that I'm sure a psychiatrist would have a field day with, the words to *I'm a Little Teapot* kept running through my mind as I sat there on the steps of the Lincoln Memorial. Proper channels had flowed very quickly once it was known that we intended to return the diamond, despite the fact that we would only return it in exchange for the killers of Mason and Ryan.

According to Nelson, Dunn and Hamilton had quickly agreed to anything to recover the precious religious icon and put off the possibility of a snafu in trade negotiations, and apparently the Metanayan priest was more than willing—a little too willing, according to Nelson—to send the wanted minions to retrieve it. Provided I was there alone to meet them.

The meeting was arranged for midnight at the Lincoln Memorial, chosen because it was well lighted and a public place that hopefully wouldn't have too many visitors at that late hour. Of course, there seemed to be an inordinate number of people there as I waited, but most of them were government agents, from which agency I don't know.

And I had to hand it to them. The agents really didn't look like agents. There was a couple on the bottom step who were taking their undercover roles very seriously and necking as if the man was going off to war tomorrow. Another couple, a little older, stood staring admiringly at the seated figure of Lincoln. Then there was a lone man who leaned against one of the columns and checked his watch repeatedly as if he was waiting for someone who was very late, and another who just seemed to wander around inside the memorial.

I'm a little teapot, short and stout. . . . I sang under my breath.

"What?" said a voice in my ear.

I hadn't realized that when I told Nelson he had the means to wire me that I was being archaic. Their little bugs no longer required wires, if they ever had. He'd provided me with a tiny microphone (or transmitter or whatever it was) about the size of a sequin that was simply tucked in my shirt pocket. And he'd given me an earphone that he swore was small enough that nobody would see it unless they were probing my ear. The voice—Nelson's—had come through that earphone.

"What?" I said.

"Did you say something?"

"Uh, no," I said, blushing even though he couldn't see me. "I was just . . . nothing."

"Have you seen anything yet?"

"No. Nothing."

Mother and Peter were waiting with Nelson, Dunn, and Hamilton in a conspicuously inconspicuous van on Constitution Avenue, which made it about four city blocks (by Chicago standards) away from the memorial. They had come to the site together in the van, and I had come to the Memorial separately in a cab to foster the impression that I was traveling alone.

"It's getting late," he said.

"I know." We had passed midnight and it was now about twenty after. "What should we do?"

"They're not coming."

"Shouldn't we give it a little more time?"

"They're not coming," he repeated.

"I can't believe they'd just let the diamond go."

"Neither can I, but they're not coming here. It was like I said, they knew it was a trap."

"Fifteen more minutes?"

There was a pause, then Nelson gave a brief, uncharacteristic sigh and said, "Okay."

But we needn't have bothered. The next fifteen minutes passed with nothing more than a teenage couple, rather the worse for alcohol, stumbling up the steps and plopping down on the floor in front of Lincoln, where they started to make out in earnest.

I think it was fifteen minutes to the second when Nelson's voice said, "That's it, Alex. Let's go. We'll meet you at the hotel."

"Shouldn't I go back with you?"

"No. We'll wait here long enough for you to confirm that you're safely tucked away in a cab, and then we'll meet you back at the hotel."

"But—"

"Alex, this might have been a test."

"A test?"

"To see if you would follow their instructions. In all probability they've been watching you ever since you arrived. Now please go get a taxi."

I dug the annoying little receiver out of my ear and dropped it in my pocket. I couldn't understand it. Nelson's idea that this whole thing might have been a test seemed ludicrous to me. After all, if the Metanayan priest had figured this was a setup and was willing to sacrifice his two assassins to get the diamond back, there certainly was no reason to go through an elaborate test like this. And again, even if the two Metanayan killers knew we wanted them for murder, they also must've known that we didn't have any proof against them. If they wanted the diamond back and were convinced that we had it, all they had to do was come and pick it up. If they didn't want to be nabbed for murder, they could just keep their mouths shut.

I caught a cab on Twenty-third Street and headed back for the hotel, still going over the whole thing in my mind, but not getting any further along with it than I had before. When I reached the hotel, the van was nowhere in sight, so I figured either they took a more roundabout course to make sure that we weren't seen together, or my cab driver had simply had more luck with traffic that the van had.

The door to the cab was popped open by the hotel door-man—another perk of staying in a posh place—as I paid off the cabbie, but when I stepped out of the cab I froze in place with one foot still on the floor of the cab. What I was facing was not the hotel's genial doorman, but one of the Metanayan assassins—the one who had tried to fillet me in our house.

Before I could loosen my paralyzed larynx enough to cry out, he said in a low, insistent tone, "Make so much as a noise and we will end it all right here." When he said "we," I realized that his partner had come up behind me. "Now, come the rest of the way out . . . that's right . . . and the length of your life now depends on your convincing everyone that nothing is wrong."

From the look in the Metanayan's eyes, I could see quite easily that he had absolutely no compunction about stabbing me then and there. I glanced down into the cab, said "thank you," and closed the door.

"That's right," said the Metanayan. "Now, the doorman is

looking over here. . . . Smile at him. It will assure him that nothing is wrong."

I did as I was told, adding a little wave for good measure. The doorman shot back a stupid grin, raised his eyebrows and touched the bill of his cap with his white-gloved fingers. *Just my luck*, I thought, *I'm about to be murdered and the doorman thinks I'm trying to pick him up.*

"Now," said the Metanayan, "we will go to our car. You will walk there with us, and you will make no trouble. . . . Walk along, just as if you're out for an evening stroll with friends. . . . That's it."

I did as I was told. The Metanayan who seemed to call all the shots walked along beside me, very close, while the other walked on my other side but lagged slightly behind. To the casual viewer I'm sure he only looked like he was having a little trouble keeping up with us, but the occasional pressure against my back told me that the reason he stayed a step behind was to keep his knife in the area of my left kidney.

We rounded the corner of the hotel and continued down the street. At first I thought that this walk seemed to be going on forever, probably because I was scared to death. But after a while I realized that we really were taking quite a walk, getting a good distance away from the hotel. They were leading me under some sort of freeway (I hadn't been in the city long enough to know which one) in the direction of the river.

"There," said the one at my side, giving a nod toward a black car sitting illegally at the side of the street on the other side of the freeway. For some reason he felt the need to point out their car to me before we got there. It was probably just a ploy to heighten my terror, and if that was it, it was pretty effective. I could feel my fate falling in on me as we neared their car.

It was then that something went through my mind like a dull ache: a talk that I'd heard long ago about what to do when you're attacked. The speaker had said that if your assailant tries to get you into a car, do anything you have to do to get away, because once you're in the car, you're done for. Having that thought come back to me caused my body to tense, which was sensed by the Metanayan at my side because he put his hand lightly on the underside of my arm, apparently just wanting to assure me that I shouldn't try anything.

The touch was enough to remind me that if I was going to do this, it had to come as as big a surprise as possible. I tried to take some deep, relaxing breaths as unobtrusively as I could, willing myself to calm down. The only way I could get the upper hand was if they thought I was totally at ease: If I tensed my muscles, they would instantly know what I was going to do. So I breathed some more, trying not to think of what was happening, as we came closer and closer to the car. We were only a few feet from it when with one swift move I did an abrupt about-face and bolted.

They were startled for a moment, then turned and took off after me in the darkness. They weren't very far behind. I found myself hampered almost immediately by the fact that I didn't know the terrain. Instead of going straight back up the street, which I was sure would've gotten me killed before I reached help because they wouldn't have had any choice but to take me out, I veered left the moment I broke free and ran along under the freeway. I hadn't gotten enough of a lead to get hidden behind one of the freeway supports or anything else, so I just had to keep running—something that I'm not particularly good at under normal circumstances, but I did have fear going for me.

I didn't think I had any hope of keeping ahead of them for long, but what I was banking on was that I could get help before they got me. As I ran, I yelled into my pocket, "Are you there? Are you still listening? Please, God, Nelson, you've got to be there! They're after me!"

If there had been anyone on this godforsaken street at one in the morning they would've thought I had the DTs, but I was desperately hoping that the bug in my breast pocket was working and that Nelson could hear me.

"I don't know where I am! Jesus, they're chasing me! I'm under some freeway!"

Of course, I'd taken the earphone out of my ear so I had no way of knowing if he was responding, and I couldn't spare the time it would take to put it back in. I didn't know whether or not he'd gotten Mother and Peter back to the hotel yet, and I was pretty sure he wouldn't be listening to this damn thing on their way back there. My only chance was that he would go back to listening in on me once they realized I wasn't at the hotel.

"*Aliens,*" I said aloud, panting heavily. *How long will it be before they know I'm overdue?* God, the answer in that movie wasn't very promising.

I kept running, pushing myself despite the fact that I felt my lungs were going to explode, and searching frantically for some sign to tell me where the hell I was. All I knew was that I was under the freeway. I could see one of the bridges across the Potomac in the near distance, and tried to step up the pace to reach it, like a maniacally determined short distance runner, not even knowing whether or not there was a way to get up on the bridge from where I was. But I thought just maybe there would be some traffic there.

I wasn't terribly far from the bridge when I finally saw a street sign. "K Street!" I cried out, and then yelled it two or three more times. "Under the freeway!"

I did my best, but if I was two years in a health club away from the lotus position, I was even farther from running a marathon with any enthusiasm. And I was no match for two men who really, really wanted to kill me. They caught up with me when I was about a hundred yards from the bridge. One grabbed me by the collar and pinned his arms around me, the other—the one who seemed to be in charge of carving—stood in front of me exactly as he had when they'd pinned me at home. I felt as if I'd been running for hours, but my whole abortive escape had probably lasted less than three minutes.

"I am at the end of my patience." He leered at me, sweat glistening on his almond skin as he extracted the all-too-familiar ceremonial knife from beneath his coat.

"I didn't know you had any," I said, attempting bravado.

"We'll have the diamond now."

He put the tip of the knife under my chin, and I could feel it pricking at my skin as I responded. "Wait! You believe in—I mean, part of your religion is Buddhism, isn't it? I mean, don't you believe in peace—"

"At any cost," he said with a wicked smile.

"Then, if I have to die, couldn't you at least let me die in peace?"

His smile grew more menacing. "You will die in pieces, Mr. Reynolds."

"First . . . please . . . just to give me peace . . . I have to know. . . . Why did you have to kill Mason?"

"Mason?" he replied, raising his eyebrows.

"The first guy. When you tried to get the doll back."

The Metanayan gave a little shrug, apparently seeing no harm in telling me since I wouldn't be around to repeat it. "We waited until he was gone to search his apartment. He came back before we were done. He had to die. We should have waited until we were done searching."

"Because you didn't find the diamond."

"It wasn't in the dolls."

"But you only smashed half of them," I said.

"We knew the type of doll it would be hidden in, not the exact doll."

"But why," I said almost pleadingly, "why did you have to kill Ryan, too?"

"He *knew* where the doll was," the Metanayan through clenched teeth. "It wasn't in the doll, so they had to have taken it out. He had to know where it was, but he wouldn't tell us. He died instead."

He died instead, I repeated slowly in my mind. *But for what? Oh God, why hadn't he just told them where it was?*

"So you killed them both," I said.

"Yes. And you will be next. Now we will have the diamond."

I stared into his glaring eyes for a moment, then slowly shook my head. "Not from me."

"What?" he exclaimed. He pulled back slightly and his eyebrows went back up. It was the first time he looked surprised.

"You were wrong all along," I said, continuing to shake my head, "because I don't have the diamond. I never had it, and I wouldn't have given it to you if I did."

The man who had my arms pinned behind me tightened his grip, and I could feel his hot, heavy breath on the back of my neck. The one in front of me allowed his expression to transform from surprise to absolute fury. He screamed something out in his native tongue, drew back his arm with the curved knife, poised like a viper about to strike, when suddenly a voice rang out, "Hold it! Right there! You're covered!"

Dunn stepped out from behind one of the freeway supports with his gun drawn, and Hamilton came out from the support on our other side. In the distance I could see a handful of other agents rushing to our assistance.

The man in front of me stood with the knife in the air as he slowly turned his head to look at Dunn, then around to look at Hamilton. He then turned to face me, smiled, and with an otherworldly composure his arm snapped backward, and then he plunged the knife toward my chest.

The shot seemed to ring out simultaneously to the man's face contorting. A spasm passed through his body. The swipe with the knife just grazed my shirt as he crumbled to the ground. The man holding me released me at the sound of the shot and tried to run away, but by that time there was nowhere for him to go: We were hemmed in by agents.

FIFTEEN

We didn't need to know where you were, we were following you," said Nelson.

We were back in our room at the hotel. Mother was sitting at the desk, alternately beaming at me and looking concerned, as any good mother would whose son had just captured international assassins. Peter sat beside me on the foot of the bed, his hand a calming presence on the small of my back. Dunn and Hamilton were both leaning on the window ledge, their arms folded defiantly across their chests. They didn't look happy.

"It's standard procedure," Nelson continued, "in a situation like that. Since they didn't show up for the meeting it figured that they would try to pick you up when they thought all your protection was gone. It stood to reason that they would try to get you when they thought you were no longer being watched."

"You could've told *us* that was standard procedure," I said a bit testily.

Nelson gave a slight shrug. "I could have reassured you that we were with you if you'd left your earphone in."

God, I hated it when he was right.

"But you did do well. You did exactly what you should have,

breaking away from them before getting in the car. There's no telling what would've happened if they'd gotten you on the road. And telling us where you were was very, very good. Quick thinking."

"But you *knew* where I was."

"But you didn't know that, so it was a very wise thing to do."

"Accept a compliment, darling," said Mother.

"So you have the Metanayans now," said Peter. "What will you do with them?"

"The one who tried to kill Alex is dead, and the other will be tried for murder. We've picked up their priest, the head of their little cult, and he'll be charged with conspiracy to commit murder, if not in the case of your friends then in trying to murder you, since he set up the meeting. The rest of them, I believe, will be deported."

"But are we in any more danger?" Mother asked.

Nelson looked at Hamilton. "Would you like to answer that one?"

Hamilton waited for a beat before responding. "I don't think so. We've contacted the Thai government and told them what has happened, about the murders and their people being charged with it. The State Department will make it very clear to them how displeased we are with the actions of their people, and that they've put our negotiations in jeopardy." He paused for a moment, then a slight smile appeared on his face. "This may even actually give us a leg up in the negotiations."

I looked at him as if he were an insect. "I'm so happy we could oblige."

His expression hardened. "There's one thing you haven't told us. *Where is the diamond?*"

"You know, you sound more and more like the Metanayans every time we meet," I said with a smile.

"The Thai government will want to know. And they will still expect it to be returned."

"Then they're out of luck. Their assassins killed the only people who could've answered that question. You're just going to have to tell them that the diamond is lost."

"You told us you had the diamond," Hamilton fumed.

"I lied."

"When? When you told us you had it, or when you said you didn't have it?"

"I wanted you guys to think I had it so we could catch the killers. That's something I didn't think I could trust you to do on your own."

"You seemed a damn sight more interested in that stone than you did in our friends being killed," Mother said indignantly, "so we used that to get you to capture them."

Hamilton was beside himself with anger; his face turned red and I thought if he didn't release some of that pressure, the top of his head might blow off. Dunn stood beside him, staring daggers at us but apparently more capable of holding his temper than his partner was.

"Do you realize how much trouble you caused us? Do you have any idea how much tap dancing we're going to have to do to smooth things out with the Thai government? What are we going to tell them?"

"That the whereabouts of the diamond died with Mason," I replied calmly.

"Reynolds, if you think you're—"

Nelson cut in. "I think that's enough, gentlemen. Mr. Reynholds, Mrs. Reynolds, and Mr. Livesay have performed above and beyond the call of duty this evening, and are understandably tired. For all intents and purposes, as far as they are concerned and as far as I'm concerned, the diamond is lost to all, and their part in this episode is over."

Hamilton crossed the room to Nelson. "Oh, if you think this is over, you have another thing coming—we have a lot more questions about—"

"I'm sure you do, Mr. Hamilton. But all further questions regarding this matter will be handled through proper channels."

I must say that I'd never been prouder to have ever worked for Nelson than I was at that moment. After allowing the agents to bluster a little while longer, Nelson ushered Dunn and Hamilton out of our room.

Mother rested her chin on her hand and looked Nelson up and down. "Proper channels, Larry? That would be through you, wouldn't it?"

Nelson didn't smile, but he looked like he wanted to. "Of course. These things have to be handled the right way. I don't think Mr. Dunn and Mr. Hamilton will give you any more problems. Whether they think so or not at the moment, they won't be questioning you again. I think they know that the diamond is lost." He turned to me and added, "And so do I." The right corner of his mouth rose ever so slightly. "Very good work, Alex."

"Thank you," I said after a pause. As I've said, I never could get past the impression that Nelson could see through me, and that feeling was especially strong at that moment.

Nelson gave a nod to Mother, said good evening, and left us alone.

It was about an hour before we would have to leave for the airport, the day after putting an end to the Metanayan menace, as I would always think of it. The four of us—Mother, Peter, myself, and the damn dog—went for a walk along the Potomac, holding an informal postmortem on the events of recent days. Now that it was truly over, the needless loss of Mason and Ryan came over me all at once, and I veered between sorrow and anger. But I think we all mostly felt a general sadness.

"You know," I said, "I still don't understand why Ryan didn't just tell them where the diamond was. It might've saved him from being killed."

"Don't you, darling?" said Mother, eying me significantly.

"What?"

"Alex, he was protecting us. He knew that if he told them we had the diamond, we would be next."

"Oh, God, I never thought of that," I said. I couldn't hold back the tears any more. But it wasn't the sloppy sobbing of anguish. It was more like a cleansing.

Duffy had stopped to give an inquisitive sniff to a dandelion, and like obedient masters, the three of us had stopped along with him without even realizing it. Mother looked at Peter and me for a moment. She smiled warmly and gave me a single nod, then she tugged lightly at the leash. Duffy snapped to attention and panted happily, hurrying along with Mother as she walked away from us.

"She really is an amazing woman," said Peter.

"Yes. If she wasn't my mother I think I'd have to adopt her."

"Are you ready?" He put his arm around my waist.

"Yeah." I reached into my shirt pocket and pulled out the diamond. I held it for a moment between my thumb and index finger, letting the light glint off of its pale violet facets.

"This is for you, guys," I said. I could see Mason and Ryan smiling in my mind's eye. Then with one strong heave I tossed it into the Potomac.

Peter's arm tightened around my waist, and he leaned over and kissed me on the cheek. "You know, somebody may find it someday."

I kissed him back.

"God help them."